I0631535

THE JASMINE BLOOM

THE JASMINE BLOOM

RAJAT NARULA

Srishti
PUBLISHERS & DISTRIBUTORS

Srishti Publishers & Distributors
Registered Office: N-16, C.R. Park
New Delhi – 110 019
Corporate Office: 212A, Peacock Lane
Shahpur Jat, New Delhi – 110 049
editorial@srishtipublishers.com

First published by
Srishti Publishers & Distributors in 2017

To Anu,
Thanks for everything.
I hope you like the surprise.

Life in a Metro

Sameer wanted the promotion so badly that he thought about it day and night. An e-mail dropping into his inbox with the title: 'Financial Controller, India'. Congratulatory messages pouring in from Stonewell offices in London and Delhi. An office party at the Imperial, with free flowing champagne and platters of stuffed mushrooms, galauti sliders, and duck samosas served by waiters dressed in the British-era uniforms of flowing turbans and cummerbunds. It was all as real to him as if it had already happened.

He summoned up these images yet again, stuck in traffic at Pragati Maidan, on his way home from the office. The driver behind him in the red Maruti Alto honked away with fervor.

What he wanted more than anything else was recognition. Acknowledgment of his loyal twelve years with Stonewell, the last seven as Assistant Financial Controller. *Forty-three, beginning to grey and still the Assistant Financial Controller.* Everyone at the office told him he was the front runner in the race this time. But such decisions were difficult to predict.

There was a proliferation of sign boards to his left. 'Geeta Coaching Centre – BBA, MBA, BCA, MCA, BE, B.Arch, B.Tech, MBBS.' 'Sachdeva School.' 'Indian School.' 'Shiva Coaching Centre.' 'Saraswati School.' It was like they jostled with each other for attention. *So Delhi.*

He smiled. Competitive. Every one fighting for space, attention. A city of ten million souls wanting, wishing, waiting.

At the Chirag Delhi crossing, ten-year-old Imran, a box of magazines and books balanced on his tiny body, threaded his way through the cars to him.

Sameer rolled his window down and shivered in the cold January air. The traffic fumes burned his eyes. Delhi, in winter, smelled like burnt rubber. "*Kaisa hai?*"

"Very fine," Imran responded, in English.

Sameer smiled. So Imran was trying his English on him. "How's school? You go every day?"

Imran nodded. Looking through his pile of magazines, he said, "Sir, no new *Business Standard* or *Women's Era.*

Wearing an oversized coat and a muffler that covered his head, Imran didn't seem bothered by the cold weather, the pungent air, or the cacophony of traffic around him. Under the flyover, beside the posters of Sanjeev Kapur selling Tata salt with a constipated smile, a bunch of ragged children sat around a small fire of wooden planks stripped from discarded packing crates, warming themselves.

"Sir, books? Chetan Bhagat, Amish Tripathi, *Wolf Hall, Fifty Shades, Narcopolis*. Good books, sir. Booker awards."

"You know I don't read those big books."

Imran flashed his white teeth in a charming smile. "I know."

"Sir, you drive car lying down?" Imran laughed, looking at his reclined seat.

"*Kya karoon.* Too tall."

Sakeena, Imran's mother, peered from behind Imran. She sold incense sticks on the crossing. "Sahib, one request."

"What now?"

"His shoes are all torn." She took off one of Imran's shoes to show him. "The other kids make fun of him at school."

It was tattered and had a gaping one inch hole at the top. He reached for his wallet and handed over a five hundred rupee note to her as the traffic light turned green. "But this goes strictly for his shoes, and I want to see them tomorrow."

He smiled at Imran. "What colour?"

"White," he said without a moment's hesitation, flashing his white teeth again.

"White," Sameer pointed his finger at Sakeena as he drove away.

He reached Panchsheel Enclave a little after eight. There was no one on the street or the park opposite their home. The theme song of a popular television soap *'Yeh Rishta kya Kehlata Hai'* rang out from the house next door. Keshav's seventy-six-year-old mother liked her evening soaps at full volume.

He parked the car and climbed the stairs to their apartment on the first floor, the coat jacket flung on his arm. Pari, his nine-year-old, was sprawled on the living room sofa, watching TV.

"Hi Daddy."

"TV as usual! Homework?"

"All done, Daddy."

"Where's Mom?"

"Don't know." She shrugged her boney shoulders. She hugged him standing up on the sofa, without taking her eyes off the TV.

Kavita, his wife, was in the kitchen, an oil stain on her faded cotton top, helping out Ammaji, their long-time help.

"Late?"

"Traffic."

Their conversations were increasingly in monosyllables.

"Dinner?"

"Later."

"Water?"

"No."

Tomato paneer, black daal and rice lay steaming on the table. A dollop of butter melted slowly on the daal. There was also a bowl of cucumber raita and the lidded box for rotis.

"Where's Tania?" When they sat down for dinner, Sameer noticed the vacant fourth chair.

Kavita negotiated with Pari on the amount of daal Pari had to eat. "She has eaten already."

The zircon in the nose ring of the Kathiawadi doll in the china cabinet glinted in the light from the bulb above. The case was full of little curios they had picked up over the years of travels in India. The Malhar musician with a mridang wearing a shiny sea green outfit, a pair of wrought iron deer from Bastar, a wooden Rajasthani miniature window with ledges, pillars and brackets carved on it, the soapstone elephant from Agra.

"Whatever happened to the rule of dinner at the table together?" he said, pushing back the sleeves of the pullover he wore over his kurta-pyjama, and scooping rice into his plate.

"Too much," Pari protested at the quantity of food on her plate, "Isn't it too much, Dad?"

He winked at her and smiled. "Yes. How can a little girl eat so much?"

Kavita looked at him. "You have to give Tania some space. She's growing up."

Tania had turned sixteen last month. Sweet sixteen. *Very little sweet about her these days though. Loads of attitude.*

"You lecture me on not spending quality time with the kids and now you're defending her. Ask her to come. Bestow some time to the family."

Kavita did not answer.

"Fine, I will fetch her myself," Sameer said.

He pulled back his chair, walked across the hallway and knocked on the door to Tania's room.

'Keep out. Danger Zone,' the sign on the door with a skull and two cross bones announced. *Of late, it did seem like a danger zone.* The marble floor felt frosty and he wished he had worn his slippers.

"Yes?" she shouted from inside.

Justin Bieber glared at him from the bedside wall as he opened the door. Tania reclined on the quilted bedspread, one hand holding the phone to her ear, the other punching keys on the laptop on her legs. She had inherited his looks. Tall, the family dimpled chin, the earnest expression.

She looked at him.

"Dinner. We're all waiting for you." He smiled.

"I've eaten already, Dad." The phone was still on her ear.

Look at her. Like she has been disturbed in the midst of final discussions on world peace. "We always have dinner together. As a family," he persisted.

She seemed annoyed, but sensed it wasn't going to be the thirty seconds conversation she had hoped for. Whispering into the phone, she put it away. Her laptop was going crazy with pings. "We don't *always* have it together. You eat alone in front of the TV when there's a cricket match on. We can't have a rule you enforce only when it suits you."

"Come on! I miss you. I barely see you these days."

"I'm busy, Dad. I have a test tomorrow. I was on phone with Shruti asking her some questions."

Back at the dinner table, there was silence. Pari, who always had plenty to say, knew better than to start any conversation. Kavita was quiet too.

It hadn't always been like this. Dinner used to be a fun occasion. The girls recounted stories of the day, vying for his attention. They raised hands for permission to go first. When Tania spoke, Pari had to wait for her turn. Kavita joined in the fun too – raising her hand to get a word in. *What had gone wrong?*

After dinner, he went to Pari's room to tuck her in. Pari lay under the covers, eyes wide open. Pinky, the pink panther soft toy, had her head right beside her on the pillow. Pari smiled as she saw him entering. When Pari smiled, she lit up the room. Her lips parted lightly, revealing the white of her crooked teeth, a half dimple forming on the right side of her face and the skin around her eyes crinkled.

He sat down on the bed and bent to kiss her on the cheek. She smelt of sandalwood soap. Her arms went around his neck. "Sleep here today, Daddy."

He laughed, as he rose to break the knot of her soft arms. "*Roz bolti hai,* even though you know I'm going to sleep in my room."

"No harm in trying." She beamed.

He switched off the light of the room and tens of constantly moving stars appeared on the ceiling. Pari's nightlight.

"Love you, Daddy!" she shouted as he closed the door to her room behind him.

In his bedroom, he rubbed his feet together to get the dust off before climbing into the bed. Under the golden glow of the table lamp on her side, Kavita was reading a book with the cover picture of a pretty girl with long wet hair. The closet on Kavita's side was ajar and rows of hangers with her clothes peeked from inside

He said to Kavita, "No news still on the new Financial Controller."

Kavita put the book down. She considered him with the faraway look in her eyes she always had when she read, but then didn't say anything. She picked up the moisturizer and rubbed some on the back of her hands. The gold bangles on her wrists tinkled and the fragrance of jasmine filled the room.

He bristled inside as he switched on the TV. *Not even a word of understanding.* The extra money the promotion would bring in would help the family. Kids' college, their weddings, his retirement. Why was she not interested? She had been his partner, his soul mate. They had comforted and cared for each other. *Not any longer.*

He was also stressed about the business plan meeting scheduled for the following day. Kartik, his deputy, was supposed to review the proposal and prepare financial projections, but had botched up. He had told him at the last minute he hadn't been able to. The finance team would cut a sorry picture. Every little thing mattered these days. The controllership was at stake.

He flipped through the TV channels and saw Kavita getting up with her pillow.

"What?" He addressed her image in the mirror.

"Headache. The TV isn't helping. I'll sleep in Pari's room."

Sure. Leave me alone when I need you the most.

Why couldn't she ask him to switch off the TV? He would. He wanted to talk, to vent, and to be heard. Too much to ask from your wife of eighteen years? This wasn't the first time either. She slept in the girls' rooms often these days. *Tania had an exam and didn't want to be alone. Pari needed to talk about a problem at school. What about me?* It hadn't done their sex lives any great service either.

There were pictures from their wedding on the wall to his left. He sported a moustache those days and was considerably thinner. He liked his present self better. Kavita's hair was black, her skin lustrous, her eyes sparkling. She barely resembled the grey-haired, middle-aged woman who had just left the room. In the pictures, they looked happy. Full of hope for the future.

He sighed.

The blue and green of the last presentation slide reflected on the polished walnut table of the conference room. The Corporate Strategy team had presented the business plan for the following year. Sameer waited for the question he didn't have an answer to.

"Sameer, what do you think? What are our financing alternatives?" Ketan asked. Ketan had been promoted to the position of CFO after Narayanan left for the rival company Pfizer. Hence the vacant Financial Controller position.

In the slightly darkened conference room, Kartik smirked, watching him struggle.

Damn you, Kartik! I'm in this embarrassing situation because of you.

Sameer cleared his throat. "Ketan, given the significance of this plan to the company's vision to consolidate its position as the fourth largest pharmaceutical company in India, I think we'll need some more time to review all of its facets in order to zero in onto an optimum financing plan."

A frown furrowed Ketan's forehead. He ran his fingers over his clipped french beard. "But isn't this what the meeting is all about, Sameer? I thought we had agreed we'd settle this today. The Board meeting is in two weeks."

Kartik grinned.

The bastard. I won't go down alone on this.

Sameer said, "I had asked Kartik to take a look. He can provide some early feedback."

Seven pairs of eyes turned to Kartik. Besides Corporate Strategy and Finance teams, Ketan had also invited Nitin from Treasury department. Kartik's ears were the exact shape of handles of beer mugs they had at home. Flared at ends, narrow in the centre. Kartik wore a black tie with tiny white diamonds. It looked like ants partying on his chest.

Kartik glanced at Sameer and his grin widened. Then he addressed Ketan, "I have done some prelim matching and my view is that the resource gap will be about two million dollars. I have worked out a few scenarios for raising funds. Let me show you some of the projections." He inserted a pen drive in the laptop and opened a power point.

What?

It was clear Kartik was primed for the meeting. Sameer had been set up.

After he finished the presentation, Kartik pressed the switch on the wall behind him and the roller shades moved up from the windows with a whirring sound. Natural light flooded the room. The seventeenth floor of Hindustan Times Building offered a vantage view of Connaught Place. A curious mix of skyscrapers interspersed with the British era buildings that were tall and white with elegant pillars. The glass façade of the tower adjacent to them reflected the clouds above and the winding traffic below.

Ketan seemed pleased. "Sameer, this is a fairly good analysis. Not sure why you need more time."

"It's…It's just that I haven't fully examined the options so far. The last two weeks have been hectic." *Bad move. Shouldn't have gone defensive. No one liked excuses.*

"Very well, let's go with this unless you come up with a better one."

"Good job, Kartik!" Nodding at him, Ketan shuffled his papers to signal the end of the meeting.

They filtered out of the conference room. Kartik triumphant, Sameer looking like a fool. Kartik had been playing these silly games of one-upmanship with him for some time. But this was brazen.

Ritu, Ketan's assistant, smiled at him, as he passed her desk. She looked good in the blue green sari.

Sameer Chadha, Asst. Controller Finance, read the black on silver nameplate outside his cabin. He winced. They had all started together in Stonewell, but Sameer had been left far behind. Anand was the CFO of a Dutch multinational, Rajiv had left for the US five years ago to a middle management position at Coke headquarters in Atlanta and Komal had found success in the online portal she set up with her husband. He was one of the oldest serving employees – along with Ketan and Ashok, the office boy. Sticking with the company too long had been a mistake. Perhaps he had been lazy – staying in his comfort zone while others sought opportunities. *Whatever. I'm here and I'm screwed.*

He looked at his name plate again. He didn't even like his last name. Chadha. He could have been a Khanna, Malhotra, Anand or

Kapoor. Nice Punjabi last names. Bollywood hero names. Ever heard of a hero called Chadha?

Sameer picked up the folder lying on his chair. Not finding a place on the table, it landed on the floor with a soft thud. Too much clutter. Files, loose papers, all over his desk. *If only Neena, his secretary, could file.* He read through his e-mails. A stinker from Corporate Strategy for not receiving any comments on the business plan. *Yeah, that worked out great today.* The London office had asked for more information for auditors. *More? What did they do with all this information? Light a bonfire?* Neena had sent him a note. She didn't understand how he wanted the worksheets revised. *God. How did you work with a daffy?* She sat two feet away from him and she thought it best to send him an e-mail.

He called her in. Neena arrived wearing her usual harried expression, her bleached hair frayed. He wondered if she ever combed it.

"Can you please move these columns to the right to display the growth in sales of each region?"

"Oh, I forgot. Union Bank people called. They can't come this week," Neena replied.

Focus, Neena, focus.

"The worksheets, Neena. These columns here," he said, running his finger on them.

"It's so confusing."

When she left his room murmuring to herself, he went back to his mails and saw a new message pop up. From Tim Reynolds, Global Financial Controller. Subject: Financial Controller - India. His heart raced. His breath became shallow. As if the air around him had been sucked away.

Knock on the door right then. Abhimanyu from the Treasury team, the office gossip, harbinger of all news, good and bad. "You saw the announcement?"

"No." It seemed someone else spoke for him. He could barely recognize his own voice. *Had it happened?*

"It's Nitin! My boss is now *our* boss."

"Good." His facial muscles froze and he didn't hear the rest of Abhimanyu's chatter.

They preferred Nitin over me? Nitin had been with Stonewell only two years. He didn't even have direct finance experience. He was so… young. *Perhaps, that's what it was. I am too old. The company doesn't see me as a future leader.*

So much for his loyalty to Stonewell. He felt as if his insides had been singed. What should he do? He could talk with Ketan, but it wouldn't help. The decision had already been made. He wanted to talk to someone. *Kavita?* She wouldn't understand. She had stopped understanding him and his problems a long time ago. He rolled a pencil between his thumb and forefinger. *Anand?*

"Oye, what a surprise." Anand's voice radiated joy.

Sameer's hand drew a squiggly line on the notepad. "Busy?"

"Actually, I'm on my way to a meeting. Can you call me in an hour's time?"

He hung up the phone, disappointed.

He threw the pencil in his hand against the wall with full force. *Screw Nitin. Screw Ketan. Screw Stonewell.*

Jab We Met

Kavita scrolled through Pari's selfies on her phone and smiled. Tens of them. Tongue sticking out and eyes popping, lips puckered in a kissing pose, making a victory sign with Sameer, cuddling with Kavita. She stopped at her own photo and enlarged her image.

A middle-aged woman, a trifle tired. There were beginnings of laugh lines around the black oval eyes, the texture of the skin grainy. She looked at her hair. She had refused to dye it when it had started turning grey. And now it was more white than black.

The wall clock, an antique wooden piece with a cracked minute hand she had bought scouring the streets of old Delhi, announced it was one in the afternoon. Another two hours before the kids came back from school.

She walked to the living room where her book collection was displayed in two built-in pine book cases. Sameer used to joke she loved her books more than the kids. She pulled *Poisonwood Bible*, one of her favourites, and opened the book at a random page. Orleanna, the mother, responding to her daughters' accusation that she never had a life of her own, but had given everything for either her husband or the girls. *I get you, Orleanna.*

The night before when Sameer told her about the new Financial Controller not having been announced, she hadn't known how to react. Should she have told him he would get it? Or told him what she really felt – that all of this – chasing these imaginary rungs of ladder didn't matter. All that mattered was his being happy, and he could find happiness in the here and now if he tried to. But Sameer seemed to live in a state of constant anticipation.

The living room was lit with a soft golden glow the sun imbued through the sheers; the heavy jacquard curtains had been drawn apart over the glass doors that opened to the balcony. The rays filtering through made a neat trapezium on the wall opposite that was full of family pictures. Four pieces of green chenille sofas – a three-seater, a love seat and two singles – faced the plasma TV on the far wall, in a semi-circle. A triangle shaped glass topped coffee table, with sleek teak legs, over an area rug of green and grey waves, sat between the sofa and the TV.

She turned on the record player, an artefact of a bygone era. Her father's wedding gift. They had both loved listening to music together and it came to represent the good times they had shared. She still had some vinyl records, carefully wrapped in plastic covers, songs from movies of the sixties and seventies. She sifted through the records and selected one. *Aandhi*. R.D.Burman. She sat down on the sofa as Kishore Kumar's sonorous voice filled the room.

Tere bina zindagi se shikwa to nahin…

She closed her eyes.

Growing up, apart from penning poetry, Kavita excelled in little else. An average student, she just about managed to scrape through school each year. With abysmal skills in cooking and household work, her mother worried Kavita would never amount to much. "Good for nothing," she called her each time Kavita showed her *Pass with second division* report card. "Who'll marry you?"

Kavita wasn't unduly concerned about her looks or marriage prospects. When she looked in the mirror, she saw a girl who bordered on beautiful. Long black hair framed an attractive face. Black oval eyes with thick eyelashes, a nose a touch too long but gave the face character, and lips just right – neither too thin nor too full. She was fair skinned, in a country where fairness was – and still is – at a premium. The matrimonial columns would describe girls with her proportions *healthy*. By today's standards, she would've been called overweight. But those were generous times; a few extra kilos were no big deal.

Her father Sher Singh Chauhan was a poet. Albeit not a successful one. His looks (six feet plus, muscular frame and handlebar moustaches that curled up at the ends), his work (he owned a neighbourhood grocery store in sector 31 of Chandigarh) and his ferocious name – all kind of stacked against his being taken seriously as a poet. So he named his firstborn, Kavita. A poem.

Kavita lived up to her name and wrote her first poem at five. About dreams turning into reality, bits of paper into rabbits and frogs into flowers that got published in the school magazine. Sher Singh, the proud father, had copies at home and the store. Whenever a customer stepped in for bread and eggs, Sher Singh managed to slip it under the person's nose. It got to the point that people in the neighbourhood started to avoid him for fear of being subjected to that piece of juvenile poetry yet again.

When Kavita was older, she got published in local newspapers, recited at college and community functions. Her favourite was Byron. The despondence and the intense self-analysis in his poetry moved her.

In the growing up years, her poetry dutifully took romantic hues and spoke of unrequited love and longing.

When the pain of loneliness nibbles at me
When the melancholy of solitude nudges me by the elbow
And I am afraid to turn around

To stare it full in the face
It's then
That I dream of you.

Chandigarh was her muse. Le Corbusier's Chandigarh. The city beautiful. Wide streets, elegant homes, the lake, the gardens. But there was more to the city than cleanliness and planning. There was zest for life, an appreciation for good things, and pride in their abode that knit its warm-hearted dwellers together.

When in college, she began helping out at the store in the afternoons – siesta time for her parents. She sat behind the counter and read; few customers came at that time of the day. She liked being at the store. The familiar sweet soapy smell reminded her of her childhood, the time spent there basking in the attention of her father.

On a lazy summer afternoon, she sat cross-legged on a chair behind the counter, sleepy with heat and boredom, listening to the gentle hum of the refrigeration. A cherry red motorbike stopped outside the store. A young man walked in, helmet in hand. Without looking directly at her, he asked for a sachet of shampoo.

"Which one?" she asked, pointing to the colourful strings hanging on the wall.

"*Koi bhi,*" he replied softly.

"*Arey, bolo kaun sa.*" It was too hot to be playing guessing games.

"Black."

She asked for a rupee. As if embarrassed at the diminutive payment, he added a pack of Glucose biscuits. He still didn't look at her, though while reaching for the shampoo above the shelves crammed with Maggi noodles and Haldiram namkeens, she had felt his eyes on her. The next day he returned for another sachet of Sunsilk Black and a pack of Brittania Glucose D biscuits.

And then again the following day. *Odd.*

He was tall and thin, with too long hair, delicate hands and a serious expression. She wondered if he ever smiled. It was now obvious he came for her and she liked the attention.

Since he didn't seem to progress beyond his daily purchase, she decided to make the first move. She had shampoo and biscuits ready for his visit. Even before he could ask, she slid the things over the counter. He looked at her and smiled – a tentative, retractable smile – the kind that can be taken back if it offends. She smiled back.

He still made no effort to talk to her. He came every day, they had their transaction and he left.

One day, as he paid, he lingered for a moment. She looked at him, waiting, when a neighbourhood kid barged in and looked at the two of them.

"*Kya chahiye*?" she asked the boy, her forehead creased, impatient for him to leave.

"Didi, two Cadbury éclairs."

She took the candy with the brown and orange wrapping out of the jar and slapped it on the counter. By that time, the young man was gone. She sighed at the lost opportunity.

When he didn't show up the following day, she began to worry. Had she put him off? Was he sick? There could have been a road accident. She didn't even know his name, where he lived.

When he came the day after, the weight lifted off her shoulders. Smiling shyly, she asked, "What? You didn't shower for two days?"

He smiled. She noticed he had a lopsided smile. As if the right side of his face was resisting despite the urging of the left. It gave his serious face a roguish charm though. "*Amritsar gaya tha*. Wedding."

"Yours?"

"No, no." He looked at her in trepidation.

She laughed. Taking out two ice cold bottles from the refrigerator behind her, she asked, "Limca or Coke?"

His name was Sameer. He was in his final year of MBA. He lived in sector 26. *Good. If he didn't come again, I know where to look.*

She began to look forward to her afternoons. He never said much, nor stayed too long. But she liked the way he spoke to her, the way he looked at her.

She wanted to show him off. Nandita, her best friend at the time, was the obvious choice. Nandita and Kavita had met a year ago when they both joined DAV College, but had become friends quickly – in their shared distaste for college lectures and preference for tea and samosas in the canteen instead. Nandita was new in the city. Her family had moved in from Amritsar that year. And Kavita had lost most of her school friends to different courses or different colleges.

Over a shared plate of *chaat paapdi (khatta zyada, mirchi kum)* at Gopal Sweets in sector 8, she told Nandita. The next day, Nandita joined her in the store, partially hidden by the counter and the candy jars on top of it. At the usual time, Sameer arrived. He parked his motorcycle and climbed up the three steps to the shop, with the lopsided smile Kavita had come to find charming. However, the smile evaporated the instant he saw a third person.

Kavita introduced them quickly, eager to get over the awkwardness of the situation. But it was soon apparent that this wasn't an ordinary awkwardness. Nandita and Sameer looked at each other bewildered.

Nandita spoke first. "What are *you* doing here?"

"What are *you* doing here?"

"Kavita is my friend."

"I wanted shampoo."

"And you couldn't find another shop in all of Chandigarh!"

Kavita looked from one to the other in confusion. "You know him?" She finally asked Nandita, as neither of them seemed to think it necessary to fill her in.

"I wish I didn't." Nandita shook her head as she stared hard at Sameer. "He's my brother."

Now it wasn't as bad as Kavita had started to fear. He was her *brother*. Not her boyfriend or fiancé. Her love story hadn't turned into one of those movies of the sixties where the heroine doesn't have a choice but to sacrifice her love for her best friend.

Nandita stared at her brother. "You *knew* she was my friend. You saw her with me and you followed her here."

"No."

"Don't lie. You suck at it."

He did.

"Dad's going to love this." She rushed out to her scooty and was gone. Sameer looked at Kavita, saw the disappointment in her face, and followed.

Kavita's love story had crumbled in an unexpected way. At college the next day, Kavita realized Nandita expected her to join in the righteous anger Kavita didn't quite feel. That Sameer had pursued her after seeing her with Nandita didn't change anything for her. In the empty afternoons at the store, she missed the cherry red bike and its rider. She missed his shy smile, his gentle voice. Kavita wanted to reach out to him.

"You… what?" Nandita raised her hands to her head when Kavita told her, "You like *him*? *Him*?"

Kavita squeezed her friend's hand.

"I can't believe it." Nandita shook her head with pity. Kavita asked her to pass a note to Sameer. A poem.

I wish you were a rose
A half blossomed dew kissed silky red rose
I would have admired you smiling in my garden
A little look at you would have made my day
Would have showered all my affections on you
Caressed you, kissed you and adored you all my life
And when it were your turn to wither away,

Would have carefully gathered your soft petals to my heart till
death
If only
You were a rose.

Sameer's unimaginative response to her poem was to ask her to meet him at the rose garden the next day.

It was a cool spring evening. The roses were in full bloom. Both dressed for the occasion. He, in a navy blue shirt and grey trousers which he thought made him look debonair, and she, in a deep maroon salwar kameez which she thought brought out her fair skin and hid some of the excess weight.

She had been to the rose garden many times before, but this was different. Walking by his side, along a bed of orange speckled yellow roses, painfully conscious of people around them, their hands almost touching, the garden seemed more picturesque, more fragrant than ever. There was no other place she wanted to be then. They sat down on the grass as the sun slowly set over the Shivalik range, not talking, each lost in the magic of the moment.

Before he dropped her home, he gave her a gift-wrapped box. She opened it later to find twenty-eight packets of Britannia Glucose D biscuits. Sameer had a wheat allergy. She smiled. *He was no poet, but he was funny.*

They held hands for the first time in Hot Millions, the most happening place in sector 17 market. Their first physical contact of any kind, a good three months after their first date. They kissed for the first time in the rock garden, a month later, as Nek Ram's statues dressed up in broken bangles and ceramic tiles looked the other way.

She loved his earnestness. His way of approaching her may have been bizarre, but he cared for her. It showed in the way he held out his hand for her ice cream wrapper, the way he looked behind on the motorbike before he drove, the way he held her hand crossing the road.

Being in love was enchanting – reminiscing about the last encounter and dreaming of the next. Dreams, he had too. And she loved hearing him talk about them. It pleased her that his dreams for the future had space for her. He had dreams of conquering the world, crisscrossing the globe and she dreamt of being his companion in whatever he did, wherever he went.

The day he passed his final MBA exam, they decided it was time for their parents to know. Mrs and Mr Chadha were taken aback. They hadn't seen it coming.

"Not them. Odd family. The man barely spoke the one time we went over to their house for dinner," said Mr Chadha.

"*Par mujhe toh Kavita se shaadi karni hai na,* not with her dad." Sameer shuddered at the thought. "I love her."

"*Oye, chup! Love da bacha.*"

They came around, as the shock of Sameer choosing his own bride wore off.

At the Chauhan household, however, there was a major *yeh shaadi nahin ho sakti* moment. Sher Singh put his foot down. There was no way he would allow his daughter to be married to a non-Rajput. He had been scouting the matrimonial columns, certain he would strike a status Rajput family sooner or later.

Kavita's mother stepped in to calm things down. The pragmatic wife of a failed poet, she realized her good-for-nothing daughter couldn't do better than Sameer. So another foot went down and the feminine foot won in the end. Kavita and Sameer married six months later. With band, *baja* and *baraat.*

Kavita Chauhan became Kavita Chadha.

The home phone rang and Kavita smiled as she heard the familiar voice. "Finally."

"Like you call me ten times a day," Nandita retorted. Her speech was like a Ferrari on a racing track.

They had continued to be the best of friends, their fondness for each other surviving their relationship as sisters-in-law.

Nandita had married a year after Sameer and Kavita. Kulvinder owned a small hosiery manufacturing unit near Ludhiana. They were a quintessential Punjabi family, if there was one. Nandita had counted four Sweetys, three Pinkys and five Dollys in the extended family besides a handful of Tonys and Happys. No meal was complete without some homemade white butter and no festive occasion without some crazy dancing. But there was an energy about them Kavita sometimes envied, a commitment to enjoying the moment.

"*Khaana ban gaya.* Thought will check on you," Nandita said.

"Let me guess – dal makhni or butter chicken?" Kavita dragged the phone to the dining table, pulled a chair and sat down.

"*Oye chal, vadi Delhite,*" Nandita laughed.

A little later, Kavita asked, "Do you miss the old times?"

"Of course. College days. First day first show of *Dil, kulche chhole* in sector 9, passing notes in Saxena's class. Fun times," she rattled off.

"Does getting old bother you?" Kavita's eyes caught her image in the glass of the dining table.

Nandita laughed. "It's all about how you feel. I still feel twenty-five."

"Are you alright?" Nandita asked.

Kavita thought for a moment before responding, "I don't know. Sometimes I feel life has passed me by. All the years gone and nothing to show for them."

"Oho ji. Here comes a major mid-life crisis."

Kavita smiled.

"*Kya hua?* A fight with Sameer?"

"We never fight. Maybe that's the problem. To fight, you have to talk. We seem to hide from each other."

"Look, I'm not going to defend him. You know I never have. But he was never the one with a lot to say," Nandita said.

Kavita's right hand fiddled with her hair. "You seem to know a lot about mid-life crises. You have one too?"

"*Nahin ji,* you know the motto here. Don't worry, be happy. And I am not talking about Kulvinder's cousin Happy. God forbid, one should be that kind of Happy. Despite all his idiosyncrasies, Kulvinder still brings home the bread and sleeps next to me. The kids may not be geniuses, but are not into drugs. I count my blessings."

"How about love?" Kavita leaned back in the chair.

"*Pata nahin ji.* Kulvinder doesn't tell me he loves me a dozen times a day. But I have no reason to believe otherwise."

"Very wise *ji,*" said Kavita, mocking Nandita's tone, "You should be a psychiatrist."

They laughed together.

"How's your Dad?" Nandita asked.

"Managing." He was doing better than managing. Kavita's mother had died five years ago of a heart attack. She had never imagined that the poet-shopkeeper, who had never cooked a meal in his life, would be able to live on his own. He had surprised her. Intensifying his involvement with Chandigarh Rajput Sabha (he edited their monthly magazine, *Rajput Veer* that carried stories about the glorious past of the Rajput warriors), he had survived.

A phone call with Nandita was generally a long drawn affair. First, they talked. Then Nandita with the girls; she was especially fond of Tania. Then Kavita with the boys – Harmeet and Ishmit. Harmeet was fifteen, Ishmit nine – exactly a month younger than Pari. And then it was the boys and the girls. It pleased her to see the kids bonding, carrying on the affinity Nandita and Kavita had forged years ago.

One of the family photographs in the living room was of Harmeet and Tania taken on the lawn of Nandita's house in Ludhiana. They are three and four respectively; their clothes are spattered with mud and grass, after having played in the rain. Harmeet's *jooda* has come untied and his hair is all over his face and little Tania is holding his hair back to ensure his face is visible as they sit posing for the camera, grinning in conspiracy.

Since the kids were away to school, Kavita enjoyed talking to Nandita without the pressure of time.

Afterwards, she sat on the balcony, soaking in the mild winter sun and watched little kids play in the park. Ammaji joined her a little later, moving the jar of carrot pickle in the sun, before sitting cross legged on a *dari* on the floor, shelling peas.

The gloom of the morning had shifted.

Pari ran through the front door and hugged her. Tania followed and went straight into her room. *Something had gone wrong.*

Pari was her usual chirpy self, "Guess what happened?"

"Obama came to see you?"

"Highest score in class in the maths test!"

"I love you." Kavita hugged Pari.

"I'm awesome. Everyone loves me. Even dogs. Bruno followed me from the bus stand to our house." When Pari spoke, her hands did half of the talking.

"Shreya's dog?" Shreya was Pari's friend next door.

"Yes." Pari's eyes twinkled with amusement. "She had to drag him to her house." Her hands pulled the imagined leash in the air.

Kavita pinched Pari's nose. "There is something about you. Even dogs can't resist you."

She had ambitiously named her Pratishta. Pride. Honor. However, the name never stuck. Everyone called her Pari.

After settling Pari for lunch, she went to Tania's room. She lay on the bed with an arm over her eyes, still in the school uniform.

Tania didn't look like Kavita at all. She had her dark oval eyes, but that was it. Tania was tall, petite and a shade darker. She almost always wore her hair in a tight pony tail. Beautiful, but not soft. She had a hint of Sameer's cleft chin. Even in temperament, she was more like him – quick to get angry, quick to regret.

"Hey baby, what's the matter?" Kavita said, drawing apart the curtains and opening the windows of Tania's room.

"Nothing."

"Come on. Something is bothering you." She sat on the bed, stroking Tania's hair.

"There's nothing. Besides, you can't do anything." She stiffened.

This was going to take a while.

Kavita wondered how Sameer would have reacted in the situation. He would have probably walked away, rationalizing to himself that he had tried. She didn't have that option. She was the mother.

She sat there, stroking her head, waiting, till Tania burst into tears and buried her face in Kavita's lap. Kavita felt Tania's pain. It had been like that since she was a baby. When Tania got hurt, Kavita hurt too.

Slowly, Tania started talking. Shruti, her best friend, hadn't been to school that day and during the lunch hour, she had decided to join Aditi, Ritika and others – the popular girls – on their table. And they had shunned her. First covertly, talking in whispers and sharing private jokes. But when Tania braved that and tried to join in the conversation, they told her off explicitly.

High school was a cruel place. As Kavita comforted her, she wished for Sameer's presence. They should share these minor pains and disappointments of their children. She didn't want to be burdened by the weight of solving these problems alone. But Sameer hadn't had any time for them for some time now. Work. And whatever little time remained, it had been golf. Work and golf. Golf and work.

She continued placating Tania till she stopped crying. She was the mother and that's what mothers were supposed to do.

Provoked

It was Saturday evening and Ritu was driving back home. A lone policeman in a white shirt over blue trousers tried to direct the traffic, with little effect. She rolled up her windows to shut out the impatient Delhi traffic and turned on the radio. She heard the last bars of a song she knew but couldn't quite place it.

An RJ on steroids took over. "You are listening to Oye FM and this is your host and dost Sanaa. Our topic today: how to keep the romance fresh in a relationship. We have a caller." A man in a girlish voice whined about his wife not being interested in sex any longer.

The over-enthusiastic response from the RJ was predictable, "Take her on a long drive, treat her like you are out on your first date and—"

She couldn't take it anymore and switched it off. *Everyone over twenty was an expert on relationships these days.*

The week had been hectic because of board meetings and the anticipated visit of Tim Reynolds, Global Head of Finance. She had to spend all Saturday catching up with her routine work.

She let out a loud yawn. She needed a restful Sunday. Perhaps she could ask her mother to take care of Aayush for the day. Or better still, she could spend the day there, at her parents' and get pampered by her mom.

She parked the car on the street of her apartment in Malviya Nagar. The seat belt whooshed as she released it and stepped out of the car. Her neighbour from the flat above, the shady-looking Ramesh ji, was parked in front of her. He eyeballed her in his rearview mirror, drumming his fingers over the steering wheel, a ring on each one of them. She pulled together the powder blue wool jacket close over her chest, suddenly conscious of the tight fitted polo-neck she wore over her jeans. She hated wearing saris on weekends. Tall and slender, she pulled off both the western and traditional attire with elegance.

"Aunty, side please!" The little boy on the bicycle shouted. He would have hit her had Ramesh ji not put his arm out of the car window and pulled her flat against his car.

"Aaj kal be bacche..." Ramesh ji grinned and shook his head.

Ritu clambered up the stairs to the apartment, glad to have Ramesh ji's fingers off her waist, when the phone rang. It was Sunil, in his usual surly tone, "Have to do the night shift today. Vijay's sick."

"When'll you be home?" Ritu asked, slowing down on the landing after the first floor. The landlord still hadn't fixed the broken windowpane.

"Morning. Around nine. "

She was accustomed to these sudden changes of shifts. Spending the night at her parents' seemed even more attractive. She told him.

As she turned the key at the door of their apartment, she looked at the two wooden masks they had brought from Indonesia – Rama and Sinta, as Ram and Sita were known there. Right above where it said Mathurs. Arched eyebrows, serene eyes, and high forehead – in a batik print of maroon flowers over a darker background. They exuded calmness. Reminded her of the good days.

Inside, it was warmer. She peeled off the jacket and draped it on the back of the one of the dining chairs and kicked off her shoes.

It was a typical Malviya Nagar matchbox apartment, built on a plot size of hundred square yards. The nine hundred square feet held a decent-sized living cum dining room at the front, a narrow kitchen and two smallish bedrooms with baths at the back. It met their needs, however. They wanted to be in South Delhi for nearness to her parents, Aayush's school and Sunil's work. However, since she hadn't wanted to let go of any of her possessions, the entire apartment had to absorb the furnishings of the much larger one they had had in Indonesia.

An hour later, as she was preparing to leave, the phone rang again. She looked at the number. Sunil's office.

"*Haan?*"

"*Bhabhi ji,* Vijay speaking."

She had met Vijay when Sunil had invited him home. He was single and lived alone. An uncomplicated, amiable guy, who got sentimental with two drinks down his gullet. He had gone on and on about how she looked at least ten years younger than her thirty four years.

Why was he calling?

"How are you, *Bhabhi ji?*"

She winced. She wished he would stop calling her *Bhabhiji.* It was so old world. That's what the neighbouring men called her mother.

"Is everything alright?" She asked.

"*Haanji...*" She sensed a bit of a hesitation. *Everything was not alright.*

"I don't know how to say this. *Kuch batana tha aapko,*" he said.

She pulled out the dining chair and sat down, her heart pounding. "Is Sunil alright?"

"Haanji, he's fine," he said, sensing her concern. "But there is a problem."

What's wrong with this guy? Why can't he just get on with it? Her heart raced again.

"There is something going on between Sunil and...Poonam, our receptionist."

It took her a moment to register what Vijay meant. Her fear morphed into anger and shame. She remembered Poonam vaguely. Plain but busty. Excessive make-up. Vijay had mentioned her repeatedly when he was drunk at their home. She had asked Sunil later if Vijay had a crush on her. He had shrugged his shoulders in response.

Vijay went on, "It's not good Bhabhi ji. I tried to reason with Sunil, but he got mad. At first, I didn't know if I should tell you, but then I thought you should know… before it's too late."

She wanted to die right then. Of the humiliation of hearing her husband's escapades from someone she barely knew. The implication that she wasn't good enough for him. That Sunil needed another woman to make him happy.

The bastard! How could he? She had lived with his continuous grouchiness, the drinking, the insults, for years now.

How long is he going to punish me for a crime I didn't commit?

"Is Sunil at the factory?" Her eyes were on the little dolls in the wooden curio cabinet in the living room. The Thai dancer, the Japanese Geisha, the Balinese bride – they all seemed to be mocking her.

"No bhabhi ji. They are…both not here."

She squeezed her eyes shut.

There had been another girl before. She had worked at the factory too. She had seen them together on his bike, acting a little too familiar. Though he had denied there was something going on, she knew he hadn't told her the complete truth.

She called Sunil's cell. It was switched off. She called again, pointless though it was. She dialled her parents' home. "Ma, I'll pick Aayush tomorrow. Am too tired today."

She should leave him; she earned enough to support Aayush and herself. There wasn't any love left in the marriage anyway.

But she knew she couldn't. She couldn't cut off Aayush's oxygen. He loved Sunil; thrived in his company.

She sat there a long time, slumped in the chair.

She didn't remember when she went to bed. But in the morning, that's where she lay, when she heard him turning the key in the door. Her eyes shifted to the clock on her bedside table beside the photograph of two-year-old Aayush. It was eight.

He came into the bedroom and was surprised to see her. "You didn't go?"

"No."

"Where is Aayush?"

"Still there."

He seemed to smell the disquiet in the room.

"What happened to Vijay?" she asked.

"Fever," he replied, taking his shoes off.

"Must be tiring – working two shifts together?"

"I am exhausted," he said, getting under the covers on his side of the bed.

She marvelled at the fluency of his lies.

He had two days' stubble on his face, there were bags under his eyes, and his paunch strained against the shirt. *What did women see in him?*

"How's Poonam?"

There was an almost imperceptible stiffening of his body. "Fine."

"How was the sex?"

"What?"

"Bastard!" She cried and pounced on him.

The physical attack surprised him. She was on top of him, trying to hit his groin with her knee. Then he took control; her legs locked beneath his, her hands held across her chest. He looked down, guilt and anger bottled up in his fists, and started hitting her.

"Bitch! You hit me? *Itna maaroonga saali…* you'll not recognize yourself."

He continued landing punches on her face and body till he was breathless. "Open your ears and listen," he said, panting, "I'll do what I want and you can't do a thing about it."

Pinned under him, immobile and impotent, Ritu cried.

She was overcome with disgust. Disgust at him, his whisky, onion breath, his spittle on her face. Disgust at her inaction. Disgust at what their marriage had degenerated into. Her body writhed in pain as she crawled out of the bed. She glanced at her reflection in the bathroom mirror. The lower lip had started to swell; there was a cut on her right cheek caused by the stone on his ring.

She tidied herself up, changed and went out to the car. The drive was aimless. All she wanted to do was to put distance between him and her.

After what seemed like hours of random driving, she ended up on a familiar route, a familiar place. The office.

Oops!

❁

Sunday. Instead of teeing off on the greens or dozing at home, Sameer was driving to work. *London headquarters and their dumb deadlines.* Driving through the Chirag Delhi intersection, he waved to Imran, who cheerfully pointed to his feet. He wore gleaming white sneakers.

Unlike weekdays, parking was a breeze; the lot was almost empty. In the elevator, the digital clock on top of the door told him it was almost ten. He should try to get out by two in the afternoon. He needed some down time. The TV in the elevator played a tourism ad for Bali. Turquoise sea, white sand beaches, comely women with flowers behind their ears. *That's where my next vacation will be.*

He remembered the family vacations of his childhood. Kashmir was his father's favourite destination and they headed to the hills almost every summer. The place was enchanting then. The serene rides in a *shikara* on Dal Lake with the boat gliding on the glassy waters, the walks in the flower-strewn meadows of Gulmarg. The air as crisp and fresh as the dark red apples that grew there. Even the food tasted better. The Punjabi dhabas they used to eat in – his father never developed a taste for Kashmiri food – with the sweet earthy smell of tandoor in the mountain air, served great daal roti.

His first air travel was also to Kashmir. Nandita and he flew from Jammu to Srinagar – a reward from Dad for doing well in school that year. He had made it to the top three in his class and Nandita had managed to stay out of trouble. They had been thrilled by the prospect of flying. The window seat created a conflict. Finally, they agreed to share it for nine minutes each for the eighteen-minute flight. Soaring in the sky, watching the toy cars and doll houses disappear beneath a layer of clouds had been an unforgettable experience. Nandita had to shove him out of his seat when her turn came.

And then guns had taken over the valley. For the last thirty years, Kashmir had seen much bloodshed; too many lives had been lost. The security situation had improved recently. Maybe he should visit once more. Kavita and the kids had never been there.

But Bali first.

The security guard at the reception was slumped in his chair, half asleep. *Lucky guy.* Sameer wished he had his job. No stress, no deadlines. Startled by the sound of elevator door, the guard got up, toppling the plastic cup on his desk. Pens, pencils, sharpeners, staple pins scattered across the floor. "Good morning sir."

Sameer nodded, bending to pick up a Stonewell pen that had rolled his way.

Besides the soft lights glowing on Stonewell products displayed at the reception, it was dark in the corridors and cubicles all around. Complete silence. No one was in. He felt even worse.

By one in the afternoon, he hadn't made much headway on the monthly financing estimates Kartik had prepared for his review. The report was due for submission to London, but he had a few questions. He called Kartik, but his phone was switched off. He tried checking into the system, but then technology wasn't quite his thing.

He remembered the conversation he had with Arjun earlier in the week. The office hunk – chiseled face, biceps and six pack abs – Arjun handled the resource allocation work in his team.

"Did you call Steven to check the budget forecast?" Sameer had asked.

"I am skyping him this evening."

"What?"

"I… am… skyping… him… this… evening." Arjun had enunciated each word, as if talking to a child, straightening the perfectly tied knot of his necktie.

Kartik and Neha looked up from their desks. Apparently, only Sameer hadn't understood what Arjun said. He glanced at Neha. She used to be his protégé, but was now fully ensconced in Kartik's camp. That was his team. Kartik, Arjun, Neha and Neena – the zombie. *Team!*

He thought of giving it up and letting the *goras* in London tear their hair, but there had been a few strikes against his name and he couldn't afford another. So, he trudged along, taking his time, looking for other data sources.

Stepping out of his room, he stretched and walked towards the photocopy room to collect a print out. Bent over the water dispenser, with her back to him, was Ritu. He liked her hair. She almost always wore it open with a large hair clip holding it together at the back of her head. Long, black, dense.

He was surprised to see her. She wasn't the weekend working type. She had an autistic son to care for.

"Hi," he said, approaching her lightly.

She jumped, turning around.

"You scared me!" she said, one hand on her heart, water spilling out of her cup.

"Sorry, didn't mean to," he said, his palms held in front of him in apology. "You here on a Sunday? What's the world coming to?"

She smiled. She wore a white sleeveless cotton blouse, a striped knee length skirt and flat canvas shoes. On office days, she dressed more conservatively. Saris mostly. There was an understated beauty about her; she looked pretty without having to try. Flawless coffee cream skin, intelligent eyes and thick lashes, a black bindi between her arched eyebrows.

"Catching up with work." She shrugged. "You?"

He looked at her face; eyes pink tinged, the redness of the bruise on her cheek. "Umm… London office deadline."

"Are you okay?" he asked, trying not to look at the bruise.

She nodded, looking away.

He took a step towards where she stood and his hand went to her wet cheek involuntarily. "Do you want to talk?"

She shook her head, but a sob escaped from her lips. Her head was on his shoulder and her body wracked with spasms as she let go. He felt bad for her. She didn't have to suffer like this. She was a good person; she deserved better.

Later on, when he would recall that moment, and he would recall it often, he wouldn't be able to recollect exactly when it happened.

He would recall that while stroking her back, he had lingered for a few unnecessary seconds. He remembered her holding him tighter. She smelled of lavender and cinnamon. Her eyes were closed and wet with tears, but she no longer cried. He felt tenderness for her in that moment. When her lips brushed against his for the first time, they felt soft. Despite his surprise, he felt himself responding wordlessly.

Their lips separated then. For a few startled moments, he realized the gravity of what he had done. Perhaps, she did too. But then just as suddenly, their lips joined again, pushing harder, seeking more. He noticed the quickening of her breath, his pulse. His hands were all over, feeling the softness of her breasts, the swell of her hips, the dip of her waist. When he felt her hand seeking him, he opened his eyes to find hers shut. He shut his too.

The next thing he remembered was her bent over the photocopier with her back to him. She let out a soft moan as he entered her. He remembered how her hand with the solitary gold bangle accidently pushed the button on the photocopier. Then it was like the photocopier was in tandem with them. Stroke by stroke, man and machine in perfect harmony.

Afterwards, he shut off the photocopier. But she didn't make any effort to move. He stood there a few moments, unsure of what to do. *Perhaps, she wanted to be alone.* He left, walking back to his room.

He recalled those moments clearly and precisely. It was just that he couldn't recall the exact moment when it all began. It had lasted a few minutes. But those few minutes had changed his life.

As he flopped down on his chair, the enormity of the moment hit him. What had he been thinking? How could he have done this to Ritu? And to Kavita. He had been married eighteen years. Not one indiscretion. It had been suicidal too. Anybody could have walked in. It was the office, for god's sake.

It was a blunder and he had to set it right. He should apologize to Ritu. He got up from his chair, but a wave of inertia gripped him and he sat back down. He felt safe in the cocoon of his own room, as if by staying there, he could shut himself out from what had happened.

He didn't remember how long he sat there. When he finally got up and walked to her cubicle, the lights were switched off and she was gone.

One Fine Monday

Kavita woke up and tied her hair into a knot. Sameer lay spread-eagled on his stomach like he always slept. 'It is my bed; no one can take it away' posture, she called it.

"Wake up, Sameer. Seven." She leaned over him. He wasn't asleep, she could see.

"Don't feel like office today," he said, his eyes shut.

She thought of Pari, who said that about school every day. Unusual though, coming from him. "Don't go then."

"Okay."

She smiled, surprised. "Will it be okay at the office?"

"They won't fire me for a day's absence." He shrugged.

Pari sneaked into the room and climbed in the bed on Sameer's side without a word. Sameer smiled and pulled her to him. She snuggled with him, her cheek on his.

"Do you have to go to school today?" Sameer asked.

"Me? Nooo," said Pari, lifting her head, alert to the possibility of escaping school. "Why? Are you skipping office?"

"Yes." He winked.

"I don't have to go. We're only revising."

"Liar, you have a test today." Kavita intervened before it got too far.

"Not important. And Daddy's not going."

"Pari, we're getting late!" Tania shouted from the dining room.

"Coming!" She made to get out of the bed, realizing the futility of her case.

Sameer held on to her.

"Let me go Daddy. Tania will get mad."

"Why are you scared of her?"

"*Kya karoon?* She's such a bully." He tickled her with his stubble, making her giggle, before letting her go.

Kavita rose to tend to the kids. The smell of frying eggs made it to her before she heard their crackle. Ammaji was making breakfast. Tania had finished her glass of milk. Pari pretended to drink hers.

Kavita asked Pari, "Did you pack your bag?"

"No."

"Mom! She's gonna make us miss the bus again," Tania protested.

"Don't worry. She'll hurry," she said as she started running the hair brush through Pari's hair. "It rhymes. Don't worry, she'll hurry, our Pari."

They made it to the bus stop as the last two kids were boarding.

Every day.

She tiptoed back into the bedroom to take out her clothes. Sameer liked to sleep late on his days off. But he was awake. Lying on the bed, deep in thought.

She got into the bed besides him and stroked his arm. "What's wrong?"

"Nothing."

Not true.

They were eating breakfast, when he asked her, "What do you want to do today?"

"Me? It's *your* day off. Movie? Lunch?"

"How about Dilli Haat?"

It had been the favourite haunt of their early years in Delhi. Strolling around under open skies, enjoying the unhurried pace of the place, experiencing the mélange of cultures.

They reached around eleven and walked together in the mild February sun, taking in colourful stalls selling handicrafts. Terracotta deities from Bengal to floral patterned bedspreads of Kashmir to Mysore's sandalwood carvings. There were puppets – the king with moustaches all the way up to the ear, the queen with big wondrous eyes, Kolhapuri chappals and Jodhpuri juttis. The entire country showcased in sixty-two stalls.

Sameer was content in following her, offering his opinion when asked. Unusually quiet. She bought a few things, a colourful skirt for Tania with Kutch embroidery, a small clay Ganesh ji and a madhubani painting of Radha-Krishna.

"You think Pari will like this?" she asked, fingering a bead necklace. Pari was into beads these days.

He was someplace else.

"Sameer?"

"Yes," he said looking at the necklace, "It's nice. Buy something for yourself too."

"I don't wear artificial jewellery."

"There's real too."

One moment he was far away, the next he over-compensated. She wished he would tell her what was playing on his mind.

The gentle warmth of the sun felt good. Another month and it would be too hot to be out. She didn't care much about Delhi weather. It was hot almost all the time. A short winter, when it got too cold, a spring and autumn you could miss in a blink. It was winter now, but there was a certain fragrance, ripeness in the air that foretold the advent of spring.

Lunch was a difficult choice to make. The galauti kababs from UP, the masala crabs from Odisha and Uttarakhand thaali – all looked appetizing. In the end, she chose nostalgia. Momos from Nagaland stall, their old favourite. As they sat eating on the stone benches in the shade, the spicy chutney making their eyes water, the Rajasthani dancers passed them. The men, with high *pagdis* and twinkling dark eyes and the women in colourful long skirts and bangles up to their shoulders. They had witnessed their joyous performance earlier.

He went to get ice cream for both of them and she continued strolling ahead. Her chappals crunched on the dried leaves that had danced their way down from the neem tree.

A man, swerving to avoid a child chasing a balloon, brushed against her. *"Sorry, Mataji."*

Mataji? The guy must be in his thirties!

She looked at Sameer approaching her with two choc bars in his hands. The years had been kinder to him. They had both put on weight, but the weight hadn't done his looks much harm. Most important, his hair was black, even though he was beginning to grey at temples. Suddenly, she was self-consciousness of looking like an odd couple – an ageing mataji cavorting with a younger good looking man.

It was nice to be out with him. *We should make time to do this more often.* She realized they hadn't talked much the whole day and wondered if they didn't have anything to say to each other or just did not feel the need to.

She got up grudgingly when he showed her the watch. The kids would be home soon.

Payal, the neighbour next door, waylaid them as soon as they parked in the porch of their home. "Kavita ji, I made pudding. Low fat with yoghurt. Brought some for you," she said, handing Kavita a casserole.

They were all wary of Payal's culinary expeditions. Always low fat. Always horrible.

"Thank you, Payal. This is so nice of you."

"Sameer ji, please try some." She fluttered her lashes at him.

"Of course, he will. He loves your cooking."

The girls were home. Pari was fighting with Ammaji over the amount of gobhi she had to eat. Tania ate quietly, her face hidden behind a book. Pari jumped out of the chair to hug them as Tania continued reading after an unenthusiastic greeting. Sameer tried to make small talk with Tania, about her school, her friends – but all he got back was uninterested short answers. So he focused his attention on Pari, who was delighted to have him all for herself.

Kavita went to the bedroom for a nap; she was tired. That happened a lot lately. A little walk was like climbing a hill. She needed to exercise. Pari and Sameer played Scrabble in the living room. She went to sleep with the sounds of their voices in her ears, still wondering what was bothering him.

Everyone hated Mondays. There were quotes she remembered.

'I hate Monday because Monday hates me.'

'If Monday was a girl; it would be that fat girl who likes horses and tells the teacher when you cheat.'

'Monday is god's punishment for what you did during the weekend.'

She had loved her Monday.

Daddy Cool

Tania jogged in the park, long even strides, her tight ponytail bouncing from side to side as Sia crooned on the iPod in her ears – 'I am t-i-t-a-n-i-u-m.'

Her mom had had a chat with her that day. More a discourse really. *Tania needed to respect her father, talk with him more, he cared for all of them etc., etc.* Tania didn't understand why it was her burden to bridge the gap between Dad and her. Why didn't Dad have to make an effort?

'Fire away, fire away. You shoot me down, but I won't fall. I am titanium.'

Five. She counted as she darted on the last stretch to the start of the jogging track in her pink New Balance sneakers; the rosebush with the pretty yellow flowers was her marker. Five more to go. She skipped to the next song. Aerosmith's 'Livin on the edge'.

She remembered seventh grade. She had scored A in all her subjects for the first time. She was excited, triumphant. All day, she had imagined her Dad's reaction, the grin spreading on his face as he read through the report card, the bear hug. She had refused to go to bed, waiting for him to return. When he came home, she waited by the door and put the report card under his nose.

He spent forty-five seconds with her, congratulated her limply, ruffled her hair and moved on to his bedroom. She had been so deflated. Her mom consoled her. *He had a bad day – there was a lot going on in his office.* But she had understood that day. Her successes, her failures did not matter to him.

She wiped the beads of sweat on her forehead. Her tank top stuck to her back. It was getting warm and yet the park was full of evening walkers. Overweight neighbourhood aunties in twos and threes, walking at their own pace. She hoped she wouldn't get misshapen like them when she got their age.

She slowed down a bit and nodded a mute namastey to Sharma aunty, as she passed her on the south-east corner of the park, besides the old Banyan tree with its roots hanging in the air. In the soft light of dusk, the little girl in the floral top jogging towards her looked like Pari. Even the top seemed familiar. As she came closer, she realized it was Pari.

When they met, Pari ran alongside her.

"Wanna go bowling?" Pari panted, struggling to keep pace with her.

"With you?" Tania asked, an eyebrow raised.

"And Daadu Daadi," Pari said.

Daadu Daadi had arrived from Chandigarh a week ago and Tania felt guilty about not having spent enough time with them – homework, tests, Facebook. Daadu had an irrepressible wit, finding humor in everything, and Daadi was very 'now' in her outlook. *But Daadu Daadi, bowling?*

"How did you get them to say yes?" Tania asked. There were no constraints in Pari's world. She would ask Shah Rukh Khan over for dinner, if she had his phone number.

"Just asked them nicely." Pari smiled. When Pari made her puppy face, you were left with little choice but to say yes.

She stopped running and looked at Pari. "Do you think Mom will let me drive?"

As it turned out, she did. And Tania did get them all to the bowling alley in Badarpur in one piece, even though Dayal, their bespectacled, perennially serious driver, was on the edge of the seat, all the way, willing traffic to move out of her way.

"You're pretty good. Drive us back to Chandigarh next week," Daadu said.

The bowling alley was packed with Saturday evening crowd. She loved the orderly noise of the place. The crack of the ball hitting the pins, the clackety clang of the gate when the standing pins were removed, the grinding sound of the ball returning. She had looked up the net on the origin of the game. The earliest form of the sport was played by ancient Egyptians going back three to five thousand years. The ball was made of corn husks covered with leather and tied with strings.

As they reached their assigned lane, Daadi sat down on the chair, her feet tucked under her sari, all set to watch them, as if it was a given she wasn't playing. Pari worked her charm again to get her to don the shoes. Halfway, after five rounds, Tania led with a score of eighty-two. Daadu followed six points behind. *Not bad.* He was back in a bowling alley after a decade. Pari was next and Daadi with her first three deliveries as gutters brought up the rear.

"It's such a simple game. I can't understand why you don't throw straight and hard," Daadu said.

It was then that she started throwing straight and hard and got her first strike. By the end of eight rounds, she was number two, leaving Daadu feeling sheepish.

"Beginner's luck," he rationalized.

She needed nine points in the last delivery to beat Tania. And got another strike. She whooped, gave them a fist bump, imitating the dudes in the next lane, who looked curiously at her. The portly old woman with salt and pepper hair. By the time they left, she was offering them advice on how to throw a curve ball to maximize impact.

Dayal didn't part with the keys on the drive back home, despite Tania's pleading.

Daadi was on a high. "I'll introduce my kitty party friends to bowling. It's fun."

"Play for money," Daadu said.

When they reached home, Tania gave her surprised dad a big hug, under her mom's approving gaze. *Whatever. It had been a fun evening.*

It was lunch time. Avantika, Shruti and Tania were at their usual table in the big cavernous hall that was the school cafeteria. Tania's veggie pizza was delicious. Mushrooms, baby corn, capsicum, diced tomato and lots of cheese. Just the way she liked it. She listened, amused at Shruti's account of her kid brother learning to skate, "…and then he is like okay – I have the hang of it now, takes a step gingerly and then falls down on his butt yet again."

Natasha and Ritika walked past them. Avantika was friends with Natasha and waved to her. They stopped at their table.

"Hey gals," Natasha said, "a bunch of us are planning to catch *Badrinath Ki Dulhaniya* today. Wanna come?"

"Oooooh… Varun Dhawan! What time?" Avantika asked.

"Like now. He's so cute in the promos."

"School?"

"Bunk!"

"How're you going to get out?" Shruti asked, looking up at them.

"Oh, don't worry about that. Ritika has a way." Natasha smiled. "Yes or no?"

"No," Shruti replied for the three of them, her arms outstretched to demonstrate reason, "No need to skip school, yaar."

As they ambled off, Ritika smirked. "I told you Natasha. They're *good girls*. They always do the right thing."

"We could have gone," Tania said when the two of them were out of their earshot.

"You can go, if you like. They're right there," Shruti said, pointing to the cafeteria counter.

"I don't want to now."

"Come on… let's not fight over something silly," Avantika said.

"And your Varun Dhawan is here anyway," she said to Tania, tilting her head towards the cafeteria entrance.

Tania followed her gaze. It was him.

She had noticed Dhruv for the first time at the basketball game against Ramjas. They won 82-79. And he had scored two baskets in the last minute of the game. He became the school hero. Hers too.

She thought of him as someone outside her league. But then they met up in Model United Nations. He was Israel to her Palestine. She remembered the first time he spoke to her. She was surprised he knew her name. Her physiological reaction remained the same each time she saw him. Quickened heartbeat, dry throat.

How could one individual have such an impact on another without even being aware of it? Young love. How little it asks. Just a sign of reciprocation. *Please like me the way I like you.*

She stole another look at him and the spell broke. He wasn't alone. Aditi managed to make even the drab school uniform look sexy. Her skirt was way above the knees, in open defiance of school rules, top two buttons of her shirt undone. She was being her flirtatious self, leaning on his shoulder as they walked together. She was laughing at whatever he was saying.

They were a few feet away, when Tania lifted her head and his eyes met hers. In that moment, everybody else ceased to exist. Aditi vanished. Shruti and Avantika also. The angry cafeteria lady and her two assistants too. It was only him and her. And then they looked away and everything returned to normal.

He winked at her before moving on. With a smile, she turned to her friends. Shruti still sulked, stabbing at pasta with her fork, but Avantika raised her eyebrows.

They laughed when their eyes met.

Pyar Ke Side Effects

I am an idiot of epic proportions. Married for eighteen years with two grown-up kids, and he had jeopardized everything for an affair. When he thought with his head, as he was doing now, the lunacy of his actions was obvious. But then he had hardly been thinking these days. Not with his head anyway.

He thought back to the first time he met with Ritu after that crazy afternoon in the office. He had resolved to put an end to the madness. He invited her to lunch to talk things over.

The familiar soya-vinegar smell of Berco's greeted them, as a waiter guided them to a table towards the back. It was mostly office crowd, small groups of executives in twos and threes. Ritu looked radiant in a pale pink sari with a black border. He knew what he had to say and wanted to say it quickly.

"I'm… really sorry for what happened," he started without a preamble, as soon as they placed their orders, fidgeting with his table settings.

She seemed surprised at the suddenness. "You don't have to—"

"I *need* to apologize."

He went on, when she didn't intervene the second time. "Crossed a line I shouldn't have. It was wrong. I was wrong." The thumb and forefinger of his right hand pressed the little finger of his left hand hard. "Perhaps we can move on. Pretend it never happened."

Ritu took a long sip from her fresh lime soda. "You think you have the sole responsibility of what happened?"

"I…"

"Or are you being the gentleman here? Because I don't recall being raped. I remember having sex, yes. But not being raped."

Sameer gulped on his iced tea, unsure of where this was headed. She seemed to enjoy the effect her plain speaking was having on him.

"You don't *have* to be sorry. I'm not. It was disconcerting the way she looked into his eyes directly.

"But it shouldn't have happened…"

"I believe everything happens for a reason. Though I can't claim to understand the reason. Yet." She took another sip of her drink.

"We are both married—"

"So I've noticed."

There was a cackle of laughter from the private dining area curtained off from the main restaurant. *A hen party.*

She played with the straw in her drink, bending and straightening it in turns. "How can we pretend it never happened? It did. We can't press the delete button on a moment."

The waiter arrived with their food and they stopped talking. It hadn't quite gone the way Sameer had expected it to. It was supposed to be over. She was supposed to accept his apology and agree to move on. *We should be discussing weather by now.*

Her fork toying with chow mein, she said, "It's clear you feel terrible about it. So doesn't have to happen again."

Relieved to find the conversation finally where he wanted it to be, he said, "I don't know what to say." He really didn't.

They had broken up.

Or so he thought.

They ate in silence. The chilly chicken tasted like cardboard in his mouth. Twice, he made an attempt at small talk but Ritu's response, though civil, wasn't overly exuberant and he accepted the silence.

The car ride back was awkward. R.D. Burman blared on his radio, *'Monica... oh my darling.'*

At some point, he realized the incongruity of the song to the situation and turned it off.

When he parked the car in the basement of the office building, she leant on his side, meaning to kiss him. He flinched. She pulled back, embarrassed, and turned to open the door on her side. It was then he pulled her to him. He kissed her on the cheek, but when she turned her face towards him, their lips met. She kissed him a second time, her lips encircling, sucking his lower lip.

A little later, they were in her bed.

What did that make him? A Mr Ants-in-the-pants, with zero character, no self-control.

The driver club hitting the ball makes a sweet rippling sound as he looks at it fly in his follow-through.

"Nice shot," Behl concedes, as they start walking towards the hole. Behl wears a golf cap that shadows his face.

The sex was good. Terrific actually. Ritu had a beautifully sculpted body. Contours and curves he couldn't get enough of. She had few inhibitions and an appetite that amazed him. He drew his passion from her and she from him.

He hits a good chip shot that bring him tantalizingly close to the hole. He should get it in his next putt.

They had their first weekend together at Neemrana, the fort-hotel nestled on a hill on the Delhi-Jaipur highway. Corporate retreat, they told their respective spouses.

It felt liberating not to be under the pressure of the clock, to take the time to explore, to become intimate with each other's bodies, desires. Kissing passionately in the seclusion of their room's balcony overlooking the hanging gardens. Making love as the lights were lit in the night and it was Diwali for the hill.

He noticed small things about her. How her lips never fully met; there was always a tiny space in the middle. How she tilted her head slightly to the right when she concentrated on something. How the delicate light brown mole on her neck breathed when kissed.

He plucks a blade of grass and holds it in the air to gauge the direction of the breeze. He concentrates on the putt. The putter nudges the ball. It makes the distance. Hole. Behl whistles. Sameer is two strokes ahead of him.

He loves the Delhi Golf Club. There is an aura of history here unlike the new golf courses that have come up in Gurgaon and Noida.Here lie relics of mighty empires, ruins which bear testimony to an age of glory. A course patronized by viceroys; where kings, or at least princes, including the Aga Khan, had bet their golf balls in matches.

Whenever he returned home after being with Ritu, he felt an acute sense of dread. The same thought ran through his head each time. Kavita had found out.

"Very late today?" She asked him last Friday as soon as he entered. He heard the sound of his throat swallowing and then launched into a long-winded explanation of audit reports, lack of response from Pune office, making phone calls without looking her in the eyes, his heart thudding.

In his mind, he played out different scenarios of Kavita confronting him and they were equally horrible. It was agonizing, this continuous state of trepidation. In those moments, he hated himself for the situation he had put himself in. Yet he didn't do anything to change it. It had become a habit with him – this aimless drifting. Like a leaf in the wind.

Ouch. The ball lands in a sand trap. This will cost him an additional stroke. Behl has made up for the deficit already. He is going to take the lead now.

"Gilli danda khelo, Chadha sahib, golf aapke bas ki baat nahin," Behl rubs it in with a grin.

He did not know what bothered him more – the fear of being found out or the guilt of cheating and not being found out.

And then Ritu created situations in the office.

They had a staff meeting the previous week. Ritu sat next to him. That, by itself, was enough to make him squirm. A little later into the meeting, when he was about to make a point, he felt her foot up his leg and froze. There were thirty people in the room and she was playing footsie with him. When he turned to give her the most vicious glare in his repertoire, she winked at him.

This was what he didn't like about their relationship. It seemed it was only his burden to keep it a secret.

They move to the sixteenth hole. It is neck to neck so far. Today's wager, a thousand rupees. The four-domed Barah Khamba with its many arches looks majestic. There is a legend about this fourteenth century tomb of an unknown nobleman. Stan Peach, one of the golfing greats, while playing here, topped his explosion. The ball rose like a rocket, but hit the dome of the Barah Khamba and dropped back for an easy birdie putt. However, from there onwards, his luck ran out. The spirits were upset. His game suddenly fell apart, his six-stroke lead disappeared and he lost the crown. Sameer concentrates on the drive to ensure he doesn't hit the monument.

Perhaps she didn't care if Sunil found out. Sometimes he felt she wanted Sunil to find out. To make him feel as miserable as he had made her.

"Lucky shot," Behl says, as Sameer hits a draw shot. He is going to get at par with him on this hole.

When Ritu and Sameer were together, they seldom spoke about their spouses. Like they could deny their existence by not talking about them.

Once Ritu had invited him home to meet Aayush while Sunil was at work. Sameer had no idea what to say to an autistic twelve-year-old and how. He tried to make small talk, asked him a few superficial questions – music, school, teachers. But Aayush responded to only half of those, despite Ritu cheering him on.

As Ritu went into kitchen to make tea, he followed Aayush to his room, where he watched cricket on TV, sitting at the foot of his bed, his legs dangling.

"Who's playing?" He asked Aayush.

"India and Sri Lanka. Fifth one day international. Two – two. India scored two hundred and seventy-six. Sri Lanka one hundred eighty-two for four in thirty-six point four overs. Upul Tharanga and Angelo Mathews batting. Need ninety-five runs to win in eighty balls with six wickets in hand," he responded in a monotone, his eyes on the TV.

Sameer smiled. Aayush knew his cricket.

"Who do you think is going to win?" Sameer asked.

Aayush looked at him with blank eyes. "Aayush not know who win."

When he played the guitar, Aayush followed note after note. When he watched cricket, he followed ball after ball. Aayush did facts. He didn't do judgments.

They watched the match together. Ritu joined a little later with the tea. He was amazed at Aayush's encyclopedic knowledge of cricket statistics. Though India lost the match (and the series, as Aayush reminded him), he had struck a rapport with Aayush.

He pumps his fist as his putt for the eighteenth lands in the hole. The head to head record – Chadha: 12, Behl: 9.

It is nice to win.

Zindagi Na Milegi Dobara

Kavita looked at the lab reports again on her way to Dr Madhur. *No, they don't look good.* Her cholesterol and triglycerides were through the roof. The last time she saw Dr Madhur, there had been promises of diet and exercise. And she had done nothing. She knew she had to – her genetics (her mother died of a heart ailment) and sedentary lifestyle made her high risk for cardiac disease.

She rolled the window down and a blast of hot air hit her, prickling her forehead. Delhi summer, at its peak, harsh and unforgiving. The cruel orange ball in the blue sky. Glistening, perspiring, sweaty bodies everywhere, crushed by its heat. Yet it was the time when Amaltas and Gulmohar flowers bloomed; a miracle beyond comprehension.

The traffic slowed down on the flyover. From there, the roofs of the houses looked like a maze, the kind she used to play with as a child with small silver balls that had to make their way to the centre together. She arrived early for her appointment. The receptionist, a slight woman with calm eyes and a single braid, smiled at her, and looked at the wall clock in the waiting room.

Kavita answered her unasked question. "With the traffic, you never know. Didn't want to be late."

"No problem. There's only one patient before you." She nodded in the direction of an attractive young woman wearing a Dolce and Gabbana top who sat with a little boy, five or six years old.

Genuine, not imitation, Kavita concluded on the DG top. She felt shabby in comparison, with her Lajpat Nagar cotton kurta and her hair loosely held in a ponytail. Kavita smiled at the woman, conveying her empathy, as the cranky boy asked to be taken home, uninterested in the colourful blocks in the toy box. She had raised children too. She was still raising them.

As a child, Tania suffered febrile convulsions. Each time that happened, Sameer and Kavita were terrified, even though they knew it wasn't serious. That's what kids do. They scare the hell out of you. You feel personally responsible for any harm that comes their way. They pull the strings of your heart, control your entire being and run your life. At one point, they grow up and stop treating you as the centre of their world, and you don't even realize it because they never stop being the centre of your world.

The woman got up and walked towards Dr Madhur's room, dragging the boy with her. A little girl came out, chattering away with her mother, excited about the candies the doctor had given her.

Kavita thought of Pari and smiled. Here was a child who refused to grow up. With Tania growing up before her years, it was nice to have a permanent baby in the house, who brought a smile to everyone. She felt grateful for Pari's presence in her life, her silly stories, amusing histrionics, and generous laughter.

After about ten minutes, the pretty young woman and the boy came out of Dr Madhur's room, the boy bawling at the top of his voice. He hadn't had a pleasant experience. *Well, soon it would be my turn to bawl.*

"Long time, no see!" Dr Madhur smiled.

"Not like before – when I was here all the time – either with Tania or Pari," Kavita replied, sitting down across the table from her.

The examination room hadn't changed much over the years. Dr Madhur sat upright in her leather chair, across the wooden table, white coat over a sari. On the right of the room was the examining bed with the stepping stool, hidden by a linen screen on rubber wheels.

Dr Madhur looked super fit – slim, luminous skin, agile. She was at least ten years older than Kavita, but looked younger. *I should have chosen a less fit doctor for myself.*

"How are they?" Dr Madhur asked.

"Growing up. Tania is in grade ten."

"Wow! Time flies!" She seemed genuinely surprised.

She opened Kavita's file her assistant had left on her table. "So, what brings you in today?"

"Repeated the blood tests after six months – as you had suggested." Kavita handed her the envelope.

Kavita flinched as Dr Madhur pulled out the reports.

"Hmm… the lipid profile doesn't look too good." She flipped through the crisp printed pages.

I know, I know.

"Have you been exercising?" Dr Madhur scanned the file, reading the last prescription.

Here we go.

"Yes," Kavita lied, feeling like an errant school girl in the principal's office. "Though not regularly. One thing or another every day…"

Oh God, why am I blabbering like an idiot?

Before joining the gym (though joining here was defined as only paying the membership fee), she was a part of this group of women who walked together for exercise in the park across the street in front of their home. However, they ended up gossiping more than walking. It hadn't done her much good, except she was better informed about the neighbourhood.

Dr Madhur took off her reading glasses and looked at Kavita. "Kavita, I don't think you are taking this seriously enough," she said. "Did you get the Tread Mill Test done?"

"Umm… not yet."

Go ahead and fire!

"This won't do. You realize there is a family history of heart ailment here."

"I thought I wouldn't need it. Was planning to exercise." Kavita put on her most winsome smile.

"Well, that hasn't quite worked out. Please get the test done. It'll tell us if there's anything we need to take care of. That's all. Are there any other problems – shortness of breath, dizziness, fatigue?"

"No." She wanted to tell her about tiring easily, but held her tongue. She couldn't take any more rebuking.

"I'm increasing the dosage of your lipid lowering medication, but you need to exercise and control your diet, in addition." She wrote on her prescription pad. "And *please*, get the TMT done."

Oh, let me be.

She sighed in relief walking out of the clinic into the waiting car. The ordeal was over.

What if I were to die? Now. Kavita reclined on her bed, Khaled Hosseini's *The Kite Runner* face down on her stomach.

She closed her eyes and saw Tania's image float in first. Depressed, sad, unable to concentrate on anything. She imagined a listless Pari, heart broken by her mother's betrayal.

It was a few days after the death of Kavita's mother. Pari had been four. They lay on the bed facing each other.

"What happened to Naani?"

"She moved to another world."

"What world?"

Kavita had gone on to build an elaborate world for Pari. Of cotton candy mountains and Limca rivers. Of trees with trunks of chocolate bark and vanilla ice cream underneath. Where angels bathed Naani in rose water, fed her candies and *aam papad* all day and pressed her feet while she ate.

"Will you die too?"

There was such concern in her eyes. Kavita realized that was the question Pari most wanted to ask. The possibility of her mother ceasing to exist.

She touched Pari's nose. "Only when you're old and wrinkly and need a stick to walk."

Pari seemed satisfied with the answer. She cupped both of her mother's cheeks. "Even then I won't let you go."

Kavita opened her eyes. Picking up the phone, she made an appointment with Sanjeevani Nursing Home for the TMT the following week.

She walked over to the balcony. The fifteen by fifteen feet platform was her favourite spot in the house. She had turned it into a little garden patio. There were *hari champa* vines on the walls, fragrant when in bloom. She had a few plants, Jade, Draceania, Song of India placed strategically to provide the green foil to the more colourful pots of gerbera, red hibiscus and petunias. A patch had been cleared for a jasmine shrub. She wanted her tiny garden to please the nose as much as the eye. The white cane chairs in the middle made it a perfect outdoor sitting area. They had had a swing set for the kids when the girls were little, but had it taken out recently. Too small for Pari.

In the front, there were two giant Hawaiian fanpalms, one slightly bigger than the other. They had grown huge; some of the fronds were more than three feet in length. Often a source of admiration for their guests. She named the bigger one, on the right, Tania and the smaller one Pari. Sameer and the girls had a great time making fun of that. She smiled at the memory.

The evening was warm. She loved this time of the day, when everything slowly became indistinct before dissolving into darkness. The house was quiet. Tania was in her room and Pari at Shreya's house down the street. She sat down in her favourite chair and put her feet up on the table.

"Ammaji, can you please bring my pen and pad?" she called out from the balcony.

The pen Ammaji brought was one of Pari's, with a big translucent pig's head at its non-writing end. She tapped it against the pad and red and blue lights flickered. Ammaji hadn't left after handing her the things she had asked for.

"Haan Ammaji? Koi kaam hai?" She asked without looking at her.

"Nahin, bitiya. You went to the doctor today?"

Ammaji sensed her moods well. She had been with them a long time, from about the time they moved to Delhi. Diminutive and reed thin, Ammaji had shrunk even more the last few years. She wore a black t-shirt with 'SINGLE' spelt out in bold white letters. A Tania cast-off. Tania had gone through a phase of shirts with words and then it was quickly over. Now Ammaji wore them with panache, over trousers or salwars – without a care in the world what the words meant.

"Sab theek hai. Bas, I have to exercise and watch my diet," Kavita said.

"Why don't you start walking in the mornings?"

Ammaji had an opinion on everything from why Amitabh Bachchan should quit films to why Rahul Gandhi should get married and have children.

"Haan, Ammaji. I'll start soon."

Ammaji hesitated a little, *"Aur bitiya, woh TV waale baba ji* says if you feed a cow two rotis and hundred grams boiled black daal every Tuesday…."

"Ammaji…"

Ammaji seemed to understand it was time to back off.

Kavita scribbled a few lines on the pad. She still wrote poetry, though not as often as she used to, but she maintained a scrap book of all her poems since she began writing.

The doorbell rang, followed by Pari's usual high-pitched greeting to Ammaji. Shreya had come to drop her off and they stood a long time in the doorway, talking. Incurable chatterboxes – both of them.

"Call me later," Shreya said as she left.

God. Hadn't they had enough of each other?

She put the pen and the pad down on the table. She would finish it later.

A Few Moments More

You knock on my door
And tell me to follow you
It's time, you say
Time to leave.

I realize
I need a few moments more
I need to see how the jasmines I planted come out in the spring
And if the amaltas flowers will be as beautiful this summer.

I need to hear my girl's laughter once more, See her smile light
up the room once more
I need to take her small hand in mine…
And thank God once more…

I need to visit countries, continents.
I need to see all the world has got to show me.

Oh there is so much I need to do!
Can't we wait a bit?
Come – let's wait a bit.

A few moments more
A few years more.

Love Sex Aur Dhokha

"*Babuji, yeh kya kar rahe ho?*"

"*Dekh raha hoon teri choli ke peechhe kya hai.*" He continued to unhook her blouse from the front as she lay on the bed. Her breasts sprung free as he got the last hook undone; she wore no bra. He caressed them, the skin soft to his touch. He ran his thumb over the hardening nipples.

"*Nahin,* please don't."

"*Chup.* Let me do what I want. One more word – I'll call the police and they'll throw you into jail for stealing."

He put his mouth to a breast, rolling his tongue on her dark brown nipple, his hand squeezing the other.

"Oh, babuji," she moaned.

"You like it?" he asked, taking his mouth off her nipple.

"*Acha lagta hai.* But…"

He didn't let her finish. He moved his hand up her leg. She was naked beneath the long skirt that she wore.

"Nahin, not there."

"You want it too. Don't lie."

"Oh, babuji," she moaned again as she felt his fingertip.

He was hard now, straining in his trousers. With a hand still between her legs, pleasing her, he unhooked his trousers and peeled them off. He took her hand and placed it on him. Her palm instinctively gripped his hardness.

In a swift moment, he was on top of her, poised to enter her, as she lay there, her long skirt bunched up at her waist, her blouse open.

"Nahin. Please don't do this."

With a sharp thrust, he was deep inside her.

"Babuji!" she screamed.

Her legs wrapped around his waist, as he moved on her in rapid hard strokes.

"Ab kaisa lag raha hai?" He asked her, looking at her flushed face beneath him, easing the pace.

"*Bahut acha.* I like this new *khel,*" she said, breathless, her hands clutching the white sheet on her sides.

He increased the pace again and looked at her. Her eyes were closed, her face contorted with passion.

He stopped.

"Why did you stop?" There was urgency in her voice. Her hands were on his shoulders, urging him on.

"You said you didn't want it…"

"I want it now. Please don't stop. *Bahut acha lag raha hai,*" she begged.

He started pumping into her again.

She came almost immediately, with a shudder and tightened her legs tight around him, "Oh, babuji," she sighed. She looked beautiful in the moment of culmination, her face alight with fulfillment.

He kissed her earlobe.

He thrust into her hard and fast, looking at her face. It was such a turn on. Within a few strokes, he crashed into her, letting go.

He lay like that for a few moments, catching his breath, his heart pounding.

He made to roll off her, but she held him, wanting him to continue lying on top of her. When he finally rolled off her, he lay by her side, sprawled on the bed.

Sameer.

In a hotel room.

In Hyderabad.

With Ritu.

He had to visit the Stonewell plant in the city and she had come along.

She had been the maid that day, caught stealing, and he had blackmailed her into having sex with him.

There wasn't a role-play they hadn't tried. She had been the strict nurse who punished the patient looking down her blouse, the errant student willing to go any length to please her teacher, the bawdy street hooker who took money before she spread her legs. Some of these had been his fantasies, some hers. But she really got in-character playing them.

"*Aaj* Charminar *chalein*?" She was propped on her arm and looked at him, her breasts visible under the slipping sheet. The sliding glass door to the balcony was open and the sheer curtains danced in the breeze.

"Why?" He was perfectly comfortable in the luxury of the hotel room. Under the cool white sheets of the bed.

"Arey, we are in Hyderabad!"

A little later, they stood admiring the magnificent limestone and granite structure. Each of the four minarets, that give the place its name, had a bulbous dome and carving of petals and leaves on them. Climbing to the upper floor, they watched the bustle of the city leaning against the cool walls, as the sun bid adieu for the day.

They wandered through the crowded street of Laad Bazaar amid the sales pitches of the shop owners and honking of motorcycles. He had never seen so many bangles in his life – glass, lacquer, metal, plastic – embroidered, with mirrors, semi-precious stones. Floor to ceiling shelves of hundreds of thousands. Colours all around, bursting, flowing, dazzling. Ritu took delight in the treasures the shops held. She had already bought more bangles than she could wear in her lifetime. "For friends," she explained.

She walked ahead and he lost sight of her. He bumped into a burqa clad woman and apologized. He found her fingering a pearl necklace, the salesperson insisted was real. Bangles on her wrists, bindi on forehead, wearing a blue churidar with matching sandals, Ritu looked beautiful.

She smiled at him, when he caught up, bags in hand. "What do you think?"

"It *looks* real," he said, not wanting to offend the salesperson who was sizing him up.

As she paid up, he marveled at her ability to be completely with him when they were together. He envied her that freedom. He wasn't able to do the same. When he was with her, a part of him remained with Kavita and the girls. He couldn't shrug it off; guilt traced him wherever he went.

"*Chalein waapis?* I'm hungry," he said.

"Let's eat someplace else. I'm bored with hotel food," Ritu said.

"Here?" He wasn't sure if there would be a decent restaurant nearby.

She asked the shopkeeper and after a brief consultation with two other men in the shop, he recommended a place a block ahead.

Mehran was on the first floor of a ramshackle building. He walked through the door with some apprehension. It seemed clean enough though. The aroma of the barbequed meat made him hungrier. A few of the tables were occupied, with some serious eating going on.

They sat near a window, watching the teeming market below. Even her faint reflection in the glass looked beautiful. A teenaged boy came to take their order.

"Menu?" Sameer asked.

"*Hum batate hain na sahib.*"

The boy took a breath and rattled off, without a pause, "Chicken tandoori, chicken afghani, reshmit kebab, chicken tikka, tangri kebab, chicken curry, chicken biryani, mutton seekh, mutton tikka, mutton curry, mutton biryani, special Hyderabadi biryani…"

They looked at each other and smiled at the human menu in front of them. They ordered lamb seekh kebabs and special Hyderabadi biryani. Their young friend seemed to approve of their choice.

When the food arrived, it did not look particularly appetizing. The kebabs seemed overdone, the biryani greasy. He tore a piece of kebab and put into his mouth, and was hit by a profusion of flavours. The minced lamb, the garlic, the yoghurt, the smokiness of the grill. He closed his eyes as he chewed. She looked at him and smiled. "That good?"

He smiled in contentment.

"It's like you are having a food orgasm."

"Maybe I am."

It was past seven in the evening but Sameer was still in the office. Outside in the cubicles, Ashok held court and their voices filtered through the open door. Ashok was the office boy who had been with Stonewell forever. Sometimes it was what he said. But most of the time, it was how he said it that was amusing. Ashok always spoke English in the office. It didn't matter if others understood his brand of English or not.

"*Toh* Ashok ji, *kuch sunaye* about the old days," said Abhimanyu, the gossip prince.

"What you want to listening Abhimanyu sahib? Mister Ashok knowing too many stories. Explaining please." Ashok responded.

"Tell us about Ketan sir."

"Or Sameer sir." This was Kartik.

The weasel.

"Ketan sir and Sameer sir, the oldest people in the office. Not as old as Mister Ashok, of course. Mister Ashok, the oldest. Fifteen years."

He continued, "Kartik sahib, Ketan sir sit where you sit now. But he work very much. Always working. Working and working. Even sleeping at office in the night. But he rising and rising in the company. Ketan sir, a star."

"And Sameer sir?" Kartik asked.

"Sameer sir working too but no star. Assistant Controller still. Sameer sir, fixed. Like a fixed asset," he continued. "Not move anywhere. Others gone, become big."

"Fixed asset with a book value of zero," Kartik said.

Everyone burst into laughter.

The air conditioning in the building had been switched off as Ashok was talking and Sameer heard Kartik with complete clarity. It stung him. Not because one of his assistants had poked fun at him. That he had gotten used to. It stung him because it was true. He *was* a fixed asset with zero value.

He should talk to Anand again; send his CV to a few head hunters. He had drifted along for too long. This was becoming a defining feature of his life, this drifting, this apparent lack of control over his own affairs.

He looked again at the quarterly unaudited results of the company. The figures that Kartik had prepared for him did not reconcile with the GL numbers. Besides, both the sales and the expenditure figures were significantly higher than the last quarter.

"Kartik, can you please come in," he called him over the phone, not wanting to go out to where they sat.

"These quarterly figures – they don't reconcile with the GL," he said, as soon as Kartik was in the room.

"Ketan asked us to add Bio-chem numbers to Stonewell's for the quarterly results."

"How can we do that?" He looked at Kartik's elephant ears, ignoring the smirking face in-between.

"Biochem is a Stonewell subsidiary—"

"I know. But it wasn't one on March 31 which is the reporting period for the quarterlies. The majority stake was acquired in May."

"Ketan's orders." There was a challenge in Kartik's voice. As if he was daring Sameer to defy Ketan.

"I need to talk to Ketan then. Or Nitin."

"They're both away. Ketan left for London in the morning and Nitin is in Singapore for training. Ketan wants these presented to the Finance Committee of the Board tomorrow. He left specific instructions to get them signed today. Last week, he tried to reach you in the Hyderabad plant, but they said you hadn't come in."

Must have been on the day he had called sick and spent the entire day with Ritu. "I'll talk to Ketan before I sign off on these."

"You're the boss." Kartik shrugged as he slunk out of Sameer's room.

Sameer looked at his watch. Two in the afternoon in London. He called the London office and asked for Ketan. Ketan was in a senior management meeting and would be available only at 6.30 p.m. London time. That meant 11 p.m. India time. He tried calling Nitin, but his cell was switched off.

Why should I care? He would have to cool his heels till midnight to talk to Ketan. These were provisional reports. The final reports will go through Nitin and Ketan. Let them check their accuracy and sign off on them. He wanted to get out of there. Out of that cursed office, that blasted company. He picked up the reports and signed off at the bottom and attached an explanatory note addressed to Ketan, Srini - the CEO and the Board.

He passed by Kartik and handed him the signed reports. Kartik's triumphant smile was the last thing he saw as he exited the office.

Rock On!

"Aayush, what did you do today?" Ritu asked as the car stopped at the Hauz Khas traffic signal. This was their daily routine. Aayush's teacher had suggested it as a way to get him to express more. It required patience – like feeding an infant morsel by morsel.

She turned to look at him. He stared outside his window. A young boy, about his age, displayed a plastic police car, whose indicator lights shone and the siren rang when he pressed the white button on the top.

"Aayush, look at mama, beta."

He reluctantly tore his gaze from the toy and brushed away the hair from his eyes. *He needed a haircut.*

She smiled at him. "What did you do at school today?"

"Aayush play guitar."

He had taken to guitar two years ago. He enjoyed it more than anything else.

A few month ago, the school had organized a concert. The children, dressed as rock stars – leather jackets, sun glasses and funky hair – had put on a grand show. He had played the guitar and sung. She had been a proud mom.

The last three years in Abilities Plus Academy had made a world of difference. The founder of the school, Mrs Dave, had an autistic child, and had started the school with the intention of providing specialized support for autistic kids. They had started with three students and now had fifteen. The school had four full time teachers – two of them trained speech therapists, one psychologist and one music therapist. Aayush's Manisha didi, a young girl in her twenties who taught music, had been a godsend. She recognized his interest and encouraged him. He was taking additional lessons from a private tutor.

The signal glowed green and she pressed her foot on the accelerator. "What songs?"

"Radha on the dance floor."

"Only one?" A motorcycle almost brushed against the car before moving away.

"Many." Aayush looked straight ahead.

"What other?"

"Rock on."

It was one of the songs he had played in the concert.

"Bas? Two?"

"Not two. Many."

"Tell mama about all of them."

She kept asking. He kept replying. Little by little.

It wasn't too long ago she bore scratch marks on her arms and hands from her struggles with him. If Aayush wanted something, usually cookies or candy, he became violent, if refused. The doctors explained he saw her not as a mother, but as a vessel to get his needs met. As he grew older and got stronger, it got harder for her to control him. He still had those moods, but thanks to the new school, they were less frequent, less intense.

Yet there were nights when she couldn't sleep, worrying about him. She and Sunil would take care of Aayush as long as they lived, but what would happen to him when they were gone?

When she was with Sameer, she escaped into a fantasy world. All her fears, her problems, on hold. A few moments of pleasure stolen from a demanding life.

They were almost home when Aayush said something. She was so absorbed in her thoughts she almost missed hearing it.

"Aayush, what did you say?"

"Mama, ask questions."

She almost banged into Ramesh ji's parked Corolla. "You *want* mama to ask questions?"

"Yes. About school."

She hugged him as she parked the car and then felt him go rigid in her embrace. She pulled away.

"Can Mama hug you, Aayush?"

"No."

"Just once."

"No."

"Only for a second."

"Okay. For a second."

"You know what? Mama and Aayush will watch a movie tonight."

She knew he loved that. In the darkness of the cinema hall, he sat mesmerized. He didn't appreciate feelings – love, fear or anger. Neither mockery nor sarcasm. He understood only the physical action, which sometimes made him laugh at absolutely the wrong places, eliciting stares from others.

"Watch Rahul movie," he responded, rocking himself, calming down his own excitement. Shahrukh Khan fascinated him.

As she turned the key at the door of their apartment, she looked at the Rama and Sinta masks on the door. *The irony.*

Sunil was home, sprawled on the sofa in the living room, in front of the TV. As always, the room was in chaos – shoes flung away, socks draping the sofa, briefcase open on the floor, lunchbox on the coffee table.

"Hey, champ!" Sunil put his hand up for Aayush for a high five, ignoring her. Ritu picked up his things to put them in their appointed place.

She went into the bedroom and discarded her sari for a more comfortable T shirt, jeans and flats. When she came out, Sunil and Aayush were busy playing X-box.

"Aayush, go and change, beta. Remember the movie?" She said, looking at herself in the mirror, smoothing the shirt over her flat stomach.

Aayush was immersed in the game. His eyes unblinking, a frown on his forehead. Doing his best to beat his father in a sword fight they had going on the TV monitor in front of them.

"You're watching a movie?" Sunil asked, not looking at her.

"Want to come?"

"No, I have night duty."

I know what nightly duties you have.

Of late, she had learnt to keep out of his way. They barely spoke to each other; his erratic working hours made that easier.

"Aayush!" she called again.

Aayush was too busy attacking the red swordsman of his father. He couldn't be drawn to the mundane.

"Shoot!" Sunil exclaimed, dropping his console. His swordsman lay on the ground. "You won again, champ!"

For a fleeting second, she glimpsed a brightening in Aayush's eyes and then it was gone.

"You want to play another round?" Sunil asked.

"Okay," Aayush answered.

And then they were at it again. The earnest, absorbed look was back on Aayush's face. She felt a twinge of envy, seeing them together like this.

It hadn't always been like this. They had been a family once. Till he decided to punish her for a crime she never committed.

❖

They returned to India after Aayush's autism was discovered. Staying in Indonesia, without adequate medical facilities and family support, was no longer a viable option.

Sunil accepted a job that offered him a quarter of what he made in Indonesia. Shift Supervisor in a Maruti Suzuki ancillary in Okhla. He detested the new place – from the potbellied Punjabi owner and his expletive-ridden speech to the meaningless office politics to the grime of the shop floor that never left his hair. He struggled against all of it every day. Ritu started to look for a job, any job. They needed the money. She accepted a secretarial position that came her way, working for the marketing director of a pharmaceutical company.

It was then that the bickering began. Two frustrated individuals coming back home after a trying day at work. To an autistic child who needed care. First, they fought over inconsequential things and then over more fundamental things. Things they couldn't change. It was about that time he started dallying with the bottle.

On a chilly December night, Sunil didn't return home till two in the morning. When he finally arrived, he could barely stand. There was mud on his clothes and the stench was unbearable. She had been worried sick and scolded him.

"Don't you feel ashamed?" Ritu asked him, not expecting an intelligible answer.

She got one however. "Ashamed? Why should I be ashamed? I didn't ruin my child's life."

She stared at him, the wind knocked out of her. "What do you mean? What did I do?"

"You know what you did," he slurred, sitting on the dining room chair, struggling with his shoe laces.

"What did I do?" she asked again, her voice high, her body taut.

"Do I have to spell it for you? Poor Aayush. Done in…by his own mother." He flung away a shoe.

"What the fuck are you talking about?" She shook him by the shoulders. There were tears in her eyes as she braced herself for what she knew he was going to say.

He jerked his shoulders like he couldn't bear her touch. "If you must hear it. Aayush has autism because of you. You consumed alcohol when you were pregnant."

"You know it isn't right. We asked the doctors," she shouted.

It wasn't that the thought of that one incident hadn't crossed her mind. She had celebrated her pregnancy with her friends, and at their insistence, had one gin. It was too early to be worried, they had assured her. He had been furious when she told him. She had realized her blunder and never repeated it. It was one stupid mistake. One stupid drink.

In meetings with doctors in Indonesia and later India, she had confronted her guilt and asked if that one mistake may have led to Aayush's condition. It was unlikely, they told her. Aayush didn't exhibit any of the classic symptoms of Fetal Alcohol Syndrome. There were no facial abnormalities or growth deficits. Autism was a genetic condition, could even be caused by some vaccines for babies. It was then she had laid her guilt to rest.

"It isn't true," she cried as he stumbled over to the sofa and passed out.

He had made his point. Someone had to be accountable for Aayush's condition and he had decided it was her.

Memories in March

Sameer pulled back his chair and stretched his long legs as the Shatabadi express hurtled towards Amritsar.

There was another advertisement for Sagar Pharmacy on the crumbling parapet wall of a house facing the tracks. The answer to all your sexual problems. This must be the twentieth he had seen in an hour. Shahi dawakhana, Sachdeva pharmacy, Sablok clinic. *You couldn't blame an outsider for thinking there was a sexual epidemic in the country and these few brave men were trying to save mankind.*

He was looking forward to the day. Reunion of Class X B of Kendriya Vidyalaya No. 1, Amritsar. Sandeep, the most boisterous student in the class then, was ironically a teacher in the same school now, paying for his past sins. He had taken a lead in organizing the get-together.

They owed their getting together to Mr Zuckerberg. It started with Sandeep finding Sameer on Facebook. Then they connected with others. Ten of them – three girls and seven boys. *Girls and boys! We all have teenage kids now.* It was Rakesh who first proposed a get together. *In the school.* It had taken them weeks to finalize a weekend. Five confirmed in the end. Rakesh, Deepak, Arun, Sandeep and Sameer.

"*Arrey, ho jaayega* return. There is Paschim Express and Punjab Mail besides Shatabadi. Don't worry." A clean-shaven guy, in his forties, his hair slickly combed over his head so that his forehead shone, sat across the aisle from him, and reassured his younger companion.

"Reservation?"

"No need. I've never made a reservation in the last fifteen years. Fifty rupees to TC and you get a sleeper."

Sameer smiled. A professional traveller who knows the Indian Railways. Sameer thought of his childhood journeys to his grandparents in Pune.

They used to travel in the three tier coach. He loved the middle berth, buffeted between the lower and upper, so close together that sitting upright wasn't an option. People were glad when he accepted a middle berth in place of a lower one. Lying there, he imagined he was on a space odyssey, exploring the worlds never seen before. The dim blue of the night light in the compartment accentuating the feel.

Fun journeys, those. Buying a Phantom or Mandrake comic from the platform, eating the packed *poori-sabzi* in a cardboard box, drinking hot milky tea sold in earthen *kullars*.

A steward came with a trolley with the breakfast boxes. Sameer unfolded his tray and deposited his, but didn't open it. He wasn't hungry.

Those were interesting times indeed. In Amritsar, on their street, only two families had owned cars. Sameer's parents didn't have a phone in their house. If his naani wanted to talk to his mom, she had to call the neighbours.

Evenings meant radio. Vividh Bharati ruled and Ameen Sayani's 'Binaca Geet Mala' was much awaited. They listened to 'Hawa Mahal' for radio plays. Jalandhar Doordarshan started when he was ten. After that it was the excitement of 'Chitrahaar' on Wednesdays and movies on Sundays. Along with it, the task of moving the direction of the TV antenna on the roof and shouting, *"Ab theek hai?"*

Then there were movies. The rare treat. Watching mesmerized as Amitabh Bachan pounded twenty people at the same time. Buying an orange Fanta from the vendor who descended on the hall during the interval and played the tinkling music of the bottle-opener striking the cold drinks.

When he saw the kids of the current generation take everything for granted – smart phones, 24x7 TV, unlimited access to internet, multiple social networking sites, he felt privileged he had seen that era. He knew the difference between then and now.

When the train reached Amritsar, Sameer was surprised the station didn't look much different. The coolies still ran into the slowing trains, booking their clients. The anticipating welcomers, noisy paratha vendors, muffled unintelligible platform announcements were the same. The weighing machines with colourful blinking lights, which gave out your fortune as bonus, were still there. As he walked towards the exit, he remembered the juice shop, where pineapple and orange juice sloshed and swirled continuously in two glass boxes. The shop was still there, though the glass boxes were gone, replaced by Tropicana tetra packs.

It was around two in the afternoon when Sameer reached Hotel Surya Residency, the hotel that Sandeep had booked for them. The hotel looked old, but clean. The marble floors didn't gleam any longer, but were neatly swept. The chunky sofa chairs could do with a change of fabric, but looked comfortable.

"Only for one night, sir?" The receptionist asked from behind the granite counter.

"Yes."

"Shall I make booking for your dinner at our rooftop restaurant?"

"No."

As she handed him the heaviest keyring he had ever held, there was a tap on his left shoulder. He turned left to find no one. Then turned right and grinned. "Some people never grow up."

"And some people are born old."

Arun and Sameer hugged.

Arun's picture on Facebook, it was obvious, was not recent. For one, the guy who stood before him had a lot less hair.

Arun said, "You haven't changed much. I would have recognized that chin and perennial serious face anywhere."

Sameer smiled, pointing to Arun's head. "But how would I have recognized this bald man?"

An hour later, they had all met amidst a series of back thumpings, hand shakings and hugs. Rakesh, the athlete of the class, was a giant, towering over them. Sandeep had expanded horizontally. In Deepak's face, they could all still see the twelve-year-old they knew. They packed into Sandeep's Zen for lunch at Bansal Sweet House. Chhole-poori with lassi, Amritsar style.

They piled into Sandeep's car again, finding it harder to fit in after lunch, and were off to school. It was located in the cantonment area of the city, a few minutes' drive from Lawrence Road.

"It must be the first time I'm smiling on my way to the school," Rakesh said.

As the car made its way through the dense traffic, he marvelled at how much the area had changed. Glitzy, glass fronted stores advertising big brands had replaced the smaller shops he remembered – bicycle repair, kite seller, chappal maker, the tailoring shop – where masterji with a limp measuring tape around his neck and a flat blue chalk in his hand, took his measurements for shirts and trousers. KFC and Dominoes competed with the old eateries – Chawla's and Surjit Makhan fish. Lawrence Road seems more a Delhi Lajpat Nagar wannabe than the market with a distinctive Amritsar character he remembered.

The absence of the kite seller reminded him of kite flying around Basant Panchmi. Sameer and his father spent the entire day on the roof, braving the heat, amidst the carnival-like atmosphere. The sky speckled with colour, dhols playing, and shouts of *bo kaata*.

As he caught sight of the familiar red brick façade of the school building, it seemed to be exactly as he remembered it. Opposite the parking, there was the administrative block that included the principal's office. An area they associated with being in trouble. There was a neat patch of lawn in front; a few dahlias were in bloom. It hadn't changed much, except the parking space was bigger, the lawn smaller. Then he noticed that the building had grown horizontally, there was a complete new block added to the south that cut into the playground and the trees where, in the shade, they ate their lunch out of tiffin boxes.

It was Sunday and the school was closed, but Sandeep had arranged for an assistant to open the rooms he knew they would like to see – their classroom, science labs, music room, the library.

They decided they would start with the music room. It had transformed. It looked very well equipped – violins, guitars, banjos, keyboards, saxophones. There was a baby grand piano set in the middle of the room. He remembered only a much used harmonium, a set of tablas and two highly sought after guitars in his time.

Sameer had envied kids in his class who could play an instrument. He was terrible at playing guitar. His music teacher had told his father with a soulful sigh, "I don't think there's a musician in him." That was the end to his rock star ambitions – live shows, wild hair, breaking guitars and having girls falling all over him.

Rakesh asked, "The music teacher, that busty woman – *Chhammak Chhallo* – what was her name?"

"Sudha Majumdar. Khai Key used to be all over her. *Tharki saala!*" Sandeep responded. The principal was named Khai Key for chewing paan all the time. The hit song of the time *'Khai key paan Banaras waala'*, the inspiration.

Even though the school was larger, the old wing of the school was the same as before. Cracked floors, ink-stained walls, hallways that smelt of lab chemicals.

The class room obviously didn't have the walnut brown desks they had used with generations of students' names engraved on it (that was the best use they found of their geometry equipment), though Sameer had been half expecting to see them. They had been replaced by sleeker fiberboard desks. However, the layout of the room was the same.

They scrambled to their assigned places. The assistant obliged by taking a picture.

The class. The room was full of memories, sweet and sour. None bitter though. It was interesting how time sugarcoated the bitter memories of childhood. What was embarrassing then seemed funny now.

"Remember the time Khosla walked into the class with his fly open?" Sameer asked.

"Everyone was snickering. And there was Khosla going on, without a care in the world, both hands in trouser pockets. *Kinetic energy is the energy a thing possesses due to its motion.* Finally it was Murali who got up and went to him and said, *'Sir aapka post office…'"*

They laughed.

"And Kanwal madam?"

"The great yawner!"

"Ravi counted every day. The record was twenty-seven."

"All of us ended up yawning too."

It ceased to matter who spoke. Those were their shared memories. They savoured them together.

"The time Virmani got mad at Rakesh for copying Murali's essay on My best friend," Arun said.

"Rakesh didn't change a word, not even the name. It started with 'My best friend's name is Rakesh!'"

"And then he had a hard time explaining to Virmani how he really had a friend whose name was also Rakesh and who was also the captain of his school's cricket team."

Rakesh laughed out the loudest.

"Not very smart."

"On the other hand, our friend here, Sameer, was one of the smarter ones," Deepak said.

"And one of the most boring," Arun said.

"Though he had a major crush on Sujata." Deepak grinned.

Sameer smiled at the memory. Sujata. Mesmerizing eyes, luscious lips and a mole right in the middle of her nose.

"Too bad we couldn't find her on Facebook," Sameer responded.

They were in the playground. With the additional construction, the playgrounds had shrunk a bit. Though the cricket pitch was still where it used to be.

"Killing fields," said Arun, the pace bowler of thirty years ago.

"Many a sporting career got killed here," Rakesh said.

"Like our Sameer here. Scared of the cork ball," Arun said, his hand on Sameer's shoulder.

"But he used to be teachers' favourite. K.L. Sharma even invited him home," Rakesh said.

"Oye, what did you do at his home?" Sandeep asked, thumping his back. K.L. Sharma was single and lived alone.

"*Saale, kuch kiya toh nahin usne tere saath?*" Arun asked.

"Deepak, why are you so quiet, man?" Sandeep asked.

"Characteristically quiet," said Arun. Deepak really hadn't changed much.

"*Bol, koi kavita shavita bana raha hai kya?*" Rakesh asked. Deepak had been the class poet.

"Actually, I've written a poem on those days."

"Let's hear it."

"*Irshad,*" Sameer joined in.

"*Nahin yaar. Tumhari samajh ke bahar hai.*"

"*Acha!* You think we're that dumb?" Rakesh asked.

"Come on, *ab to sunaani padegi. Hamari izzat ka maamla hai,*" Sandeep insisted.

"Later."

"*Chalo*, till then, listen to my *sher*," Arun said.

"You and poetry? *Yeh haadsa kab hua?*" Sandeep asked.

"*Irshad.*"

"*Usko barson baad khush dekha to khayal aaya...*
Usko barson baad khush dekha to khayal aaya...
Ke kaash maine usey pehle chhor diya hota."

"*Wah, wah, kya* twist *hai*," Rakesh said.

The conversation flowed seamlessly. Sameer hadn't laughed as much in a long time. They carried on with the tour, the labs, teacher's lounge, the principal's office, reliving memories, till it was dusk and Mahesh, the school attendant fidgety. They were lost in time, the time lost on them.

In the evening, they got together for drinks and dinner at Crystal Restaurant and recounted their present. Five middle-aged men, graying, balding, and expanding in the middle. Sandeep and Deepak taught in different schools of Kendriya Vidyalaya Sangathan. Rakesh worked for the health department of Government of Haryana, a little evasive about his work. Arun worked for Citibank in Chandigarh.

Sameer noticed the mood shift when they talked of their present. They were aware of having taken different roads, of having reached different destinations. The conversation became constricted, self-conscious, the camaraderie of the morning slipping away.

"Deepak, *ab toh suna de yaar*," Rakesh said, shifting the conversation back to the past.

"*Theek hai,* but listen seriously. No jokes."

"Okay."

"*Hindi mein hai.*"

"*Pata hai saale, tere se angrezi ki asha thode hi hai.*"

Deepak began, "The title is '*Yeh Baat Un Dinon ki hai.*'

"*Wah, wah!*"

"*Chup, chup. Naraaz ho jaayega,*" Rakesh said, a finger on his lips.

Deepak began reciting the poem.

"*Yeh baat un dinon ki hai*
Jab ghaas ka rang kuch zyada gehra tha,
Aasmaan thoda zyada neela
Aur hawa mein ek khushboo si raha karti thi.

Jab thoda hi bahut tha
Tumhein dekhna aur tumhara dekhna
Tumhari ek muskurahat
Tumse milne ka khayal
Bus inhi se mann behal jaata tha

Ab jab haqiqat ki zindagi basar kar raha hoon
To lagta hi nahin ke who mein tha
…aur woh tum.

Khwabon se ab dil nahin bharta
Bahut kuchh, bahut kuchh ki talash rehti hai hamesha
Ek bhatakna hamesha ka

Magar phir bhi yaad bahut aate hai woh din
Woh khawabon ke din
Woh khwab se din."

We Are Family

The sand beneath Sameer's bare feet felt good. A granular massage from below as the waves lapped at his ankles. He couldn't believe he was there. *In Bali.* And it was every bit as enchanting as the TV promos had promised. The blue green water, the wide expanse of soft sand, palms rustling in the wind. He closed his eyes and felt the mist of a big wave on his face.

Taking time off from office hadn't been easy. Nitin had demurred – inappropriate timing, the public issue coming up, etc. But Sameer had persisted.

"Dad!"

A *gori* teenager walked towards him holding a surfboard in her hands, a plastic string tying it to her ankle. For a moment, he stood confused till he located the origin of the voice. Pari ran towards him, pigtails flying, just behind the girl, with Tania following her.

"Let's go." Pari was panting as she caught up with him, hands on her boney little girl knees.

"Where?"

"You promised."

"What do you say, Tania?" he asked.

"I say… a promise is a promise," Tania replied, rubbing Pari's cheek.

He kissed Pari's forehead. "Right then. This afternoon."

"Yes!" Pari whooped.

Water sports. He *had* promised.

"Who's going to break it to your mom?"

Kavita was unlikely to be ecstatic about the prospect of being on a speed boat in the middle of the ocean.

"I will," Pari responded.

"Be gentle." He tousled her hair.

He watched the girls run to Kavita, who lay on the lounger under the shade of a Salak palm.

The day before, he had taken the girls snorkeling while Kavita stayed back for a Balinese massage. They had paired off: the guide and Pari, Tania and him. As they glided through the luminescent corrals, that swayed one way and then the other, in a rhythmic motion, playing to the unheard music of the sea, they had bonded somewhat. At least, for some time, her sullen teenage exterior had crumbled, and she had become his little girl once again.

He felt hot in the sun. Perhaps he should go back and lie down in the shade. But a swim first. He waded into the sea, almost to his chest. The sea, undulating, heaving gently. He dived, riding the waves.

Their hotel stood on a private beach. They had a clear view of the Indian Ocean from the balcony of their room and heard the waves crashing in the night. The large manicured grounds were dotted with palms, flowering frangipani, and mango trees so laden with fruit that it almost touched the ground. A painting of a thousand shades of green.

Kavita was dozing, her book on her stomach, but woke up as he approached. "How was the swim?"

"Incredible. You should go too."

"Later..." she said, as she closed her eyes again.

He looked at her sleeping. As the wind moved the palm leaves above, light and shadow chased each other on her face. She had been self-conscious in the swim suit in the morning and wanted to change back into shorts. But he had insisted, "Come on! We are in Bali."

He felt a sudden surge of guilt. *What am I doing to her? What has she done to deserve it?* That's how it was with guilt. You thought you had made peace with it, learned to live with it, but then it struck unexpectedly, making you feel miserable all over again.

He looked around for Tania and Pari on the beach. Panicking for a moment, not finding them, he sighted them together, stick figures in the distance, jumping the waves. They went forward a few steps, and then retreated as the sea pushed them back.

He closed his eyes and then stretched his hand seeking hers. He drifted to sleep like that, holding her hand, listening to the sound of waves, the sea breeze playing in his hair.

Pari left first. They watched her take flight, as the motor boat pulled away at the tow rope. Her hands clutched the harness. She let out a scream. Excitement, fear or both.

He turned to Tania and grinned.

"The poor guy! He's going to get his eardrums shattered," she said of the instructor who had flown with Pari.

He watched, shading his eyes from the sun, as the red and white parachute soared in the sky.

They had come parasailing after a spin on the banana boat. Despite all her protests, Kavita was made to join the ride. It was a family experience and she had to be a part of it, they had told her.

The red and white parachute was a tiny speck on the horizon now.

"I'm not going. There's nothing about family experience in this one." Kavita joined them, as they looked up together.

"We'll see about that." He exchanged a smile with Tania.

Pari couldn't stop gushing when she landed. "It is sooo much fun. You are… like flying."

Tania went next. A reluctant Kavita followed her.

He went in the end. When he was up in the air, he experienced a tranquility he hadn't known before. He was alone – the sky above and the sea below. Free. When it was time to return, an unexplained sense of loss overwhelmed him. However, as his feet hit the ground and the girls rushed towards him, he felt better. He had returned to his family.

Their last night in Bali, they had done a quick family poll of the most memorable sights of the trip. Kavita had voted for the walk amongst the terraced rice fields of Ubud. It had drizzled a bit, but it had added to the charm of that emerald ocean. When the wind blew, the waves of tender rice stalks made beautiful patterns. Tania voted for snorkeling and Pari, predictably, for the banana boat ride. He chose the sunset at Tanah Lot temple. From the top of the cliff, they had watched the sun set the ocean aflame.

He felt they had reconnected as a family. With Tania particularly, he felt a barrier had been breached. For the first time in months, they were joking and laughing together.

He looked at her now, sitting by his side, watching the sun go down. He had insisted Tania choose a place for dinner that day. After a discussion with the hotel concierge, she had selected this place. It was a restaurant in Jimbaran bay called Blue Marlin. It was a picturesque area, a row of open air restaurants by the beach offering fresh seafood and a view of the sunset. Candles were beginning to be lighted on the tables all around and the aroma of grilled seafood permeated the air.

A family of four occupied the table beside them. All of them, the father, the mother and the two teenage sons were peering into their phones, oblivious to the charm of the scene around them.

The musicians who had been playing for some time approached their table and asked them if they had any requests. They looked at each other, lost for choice. The lead singer, a stocky guy with a light beard, whispered to his two fellow musicians and they began. *"Tum paas aaye...."* They sang the full song *Kuch kuch hota Hai* in an Indonesian accent as the four of them listened, amused. This was the third time they had heard the song in Bali. Indian movies, he realized, were the most potent ambassadors of India.

After dinner, Kavita and Pari went to dip their feet in the sea. He could hear Pari squealing over the sound of the waves.

Kavita and Pari were making their way back to the table as he returned from the restroom.

Tania got up with a jerk and looked at Kavita. "Shall we leave?"

Kavita nodded. "Are you alright?"

"Yeah."

Late in the night, when everyone was asleep, Sameer checked his phone. Pari's selfies welcomed him. On the beach with shells in the hands; in the snorkeling gear; with the parasailing guide; a jumbo shrimp from the restaurant in her hand and her face in mock fear. He checked his messages. No new ones. He was about to switch off the phone when his eyes caught Ritu's name. There was one from her. *And it had been read.* He sat upright.

He looked at the time of receipt. 7.17 p.m. *So, towards the end of dinner.* But he had held on to the phone all the time.

Slowly he put the puzzle together. He had gone to the washroom after dinner. Tania was the only one at the table. *It had to be Tania.* That also explained Tania's jumpy behaviour towards the end of the evening.

He read the message again. Two simple lines.

Miss you. Can't wait to see you tomorrow.

He looked at Kavita. She seemed to be in deep sleep, her body rising and falling evenly, unaware of the turmoil that was to hit their lives soon.

"Not sleeping?" she asked, groggy with sleep, as he hugged her from behind.

"Can't."

"Don't worry too much," she said, turning to his side.

He lay down with his arms around her, his face buried in her bosom. Sometime in the night, he didn't know when, calmed by her even breathing, he also fell asleep.

He dreamt of Ketan and Ritu lying together on the beach; Ketan's hand wedged possessively between her legs. Ritu smiled at Sameer as if that was normal. Then Sunil attacked him from behind and choked him. He wanted to shout for help, to call out to Kavita. But he couldn't. His voice died in his throat.

Masti

The sari-clad heroine pleaded with the hero, but no one heard what she said. The sound of the TV had been muted. They heard Tania's voice instead. "I'm sorry. Please forgive me I ate all the *amrood*."

The scene shifted to the hero, angry and stern. Harmeet played the hero's part. "Oye, how could you? What will I eat now?"

Harmeet's gruff Punjabi accent as a voice-over for the candy-face hero of the soap was so comical that Tania burst out laughing. The camera was back on the still-pleading heroine touching her belly, evidently to remind him of the life within.

"God has already punished me. See, my tummy's aching," Tania said.

The camera shifted back to the hero, who was apparently unmoved.

"No, no, no. I can't forgive you. You always eat everything. You even finished last night's left-over butter chicken. Look at my face... I am starving. And your tummy looks... full."

The camera moved to the eternal soap vamp – all ritzy, all evil. Pari decided to pipe in, "*Dekha?* Didn't I say amrood will make trouble?"

They laughed together and Nandita bua, who till then had been shouting at Harmeet to give her the TV remote, joined them, as the credits rolled down. *"Oye, khotey, saara* episode *kharab kar diya."*

"Bua, we entertained you better than this stupid serial. Wasn't this more fun?" Tania asked, leaning on Nandita bua on the sofa.

"That it was."

"All this talk of food has made me hungry," Harmeet said.

"You're always hungry," Bua said, hitting him playfully on his head. He sat on the carpet at her feet.

Harmeet said, "Tania, when Dad asks you today, tell him you want to have Chinese, okay? And say you're really hungry. *Tere bahane,* we'll also get good food."

"Haan, like we starve you otherwise," Nandita bua said.

"Roz aloo gobhi khilate ho."

Bua smacked him on his head again. "Homework?"

"All done – *bas* maths *karna hai.* These maths teachers are all crazy. They have been looking for X for so many years, but have still not found it."

Tania had been in Ludhiana for three days. Mom had been surprised when she said she would like to spend the last week of summer her vacation with Nandita bua in Ludhiana, immediately after their trip to Bali. But then had agreed. She needed the time away from home to sort out the tumult in her mind.

Tania wished she hadn't read the message on her Dad's phone. She didn't know how to deal with what she thought was going on.

Ludhiana had been a distraction. Nandita bua and Kulvinder uncle had welcomed Pari and her with open arms. Every day, when Kulvinder uncle got back from office, the first thing he did was ask Tania and Pari what they wanted to do in the evening. She had been surprised at his liveliness; he never seemed tired.

There was a unique disorderliness about Nandita bua's home that added to its charm. Passports lay amongst a stack of old magazines, Ishmit's long abandoned toy gun in the display case in the living room, bua's medication in the bathroom, her bindi packet in the pantry closet of the kitchen. Once put in the inappropriate location, these things became a part of the landscape of that room. So unlike the symmetry of their home.

"We should leave tomorrow or the day after. School will start next week," Tania said.

"It's Kulvinder uncle's birthday the day after. *Uske baad chale jaana*," Nandita bua said.

Why not? The thought of returning home wasn't too pleasant.

Kulvinder uncle's birthday party was a grand affair. The lawn in front of the house sparkled with colourful lights. The neighbourhood aunties came decked in shimmering suits and saris, bearing the weight of gold on their weighty bodies. The men, almost uniformly potbellied, were resplendent in their colourful kurtas.

She dressed up too, in a crimson and gold churidar suit bua bought her, matching bindi and lip gloss, her hair open, falling to her shoulders. She was in the kitchen, rolling dough for puris along with Nandita bua, listening to the conversation around her.

"Navjot, are these earrings new?"

"*Haanji*, rubies. *Karnal waale mamaji ne diye hain* gift."

Pinky aunty, Bua's next door neighbour of enormous proportions, held Tania's wrist. "*Kudi toh sohni hai, par patli bahut hai. Khaana nahin khilate tere* mummy daddy?"

"*Nahin, aunty ji, bahut gareeb hain. Mamaji* postman *hain, zyada kamai nahin hoti*," Harmeet responded on her behalf, grabbing a plate of samosas from the kitchen island.

Pinky aunty thumped his back in response as they all laughed.

"*Khul ke hasa kar*," Pinky aunty advised her, her gigantic breasts thrust in Tania's face.

Tania took platters of salted cashews and samosas for the men in the living room. One of Harmeet's friends in a dandy blue suit, waylaid her on the lawn, striking a pose, a hand on the wall. "Hello ji."

Harmeet, right behind him, smacked him on his head. "Oye, *panga nahin. Behan hai meri.*"

Some of the men were in deep conversation, drinks in hand, as filmi ghazals played in the background. Pinky aunty harangued her husband, "*Haanji, kinne peg ho gaye?*"

"*Dooja hi hai ji.*"

"I know – *tuhanu ginti do tak hi aandi hai.* One. Two. Two. Two. Two."

Bhatia uncle, another neighbour of theirs, swooned over the song. "Lyrics *suno ji. Kya baat hai. Ek tu hi dhanwaan hai gori, baaki sab kangaal.* Correct *hai ji. Wah wah.*"

"Lyrics *toh* old songs *ke hi hote the ji. Ab to bas kabhi* Jhandu balm *hai toh kabhi* Fevicol," his companion, a sardarji with a perfect circle face covered in dyed beard, responded.

Bhatia uncle smiled at her in recognition, when she reached him. "*Puttar ji, aapne kuch khaaya ke nahin? Khaane ki sab se zyada zaroorat toh aap ko hai.*"

Kulvinder uncle smiled, took the tray from her, and stuffed a samosa in her mouth, "*Bilkul. Hum ne ek hafte mein isko tagda karke bhejna hai Delhi.*"

A sardarji, with a Santa Claus beard, had a motley audience in the porch, hanging on to his words. "Some hope from this Government. *Sardar ji ney te kujh kitta hi nahin, bas hath bun ke khade rahe* madam *de saamne.*"

On her way back to kitchen, she caught the dandy blue suit chatting up a pretty girl in a yellow salwar suit on the lawn, who was aflutter with the attention.

Pari came sprinting and held her by the legs, her lehenga suit awry, her hair messed up, with a little girl in hot pursuit. Apparently, it was a game Pari had invented. Pari was safe as long as she was touching another human. The little girl stood patiently, waiting for her to let go of Tania.

"Come inside. Let me re-do your hair, stupid." Tania herded her inside.

In the kitchen, the ladies were done with the cooking and keen to feed the men, as Pinky aunty prophesied, "*Nahin te aina da peena bund nahin hona.* Capacity *hai nahin, shauq bahut hai.*"

The night reached its crescendo after dinner, when the dancing began in the living room, the furniture moved aside to make space. It started with the younger crowd, teenage boys and girls, but then, as the music changed from Bollywood to Punjabi, the ladies got pulled in and then they ensured the men shook a leg too.

Dandy blue suit turned out to be a fantastic dancer and made a great pair with the yellow salwar suit. Harmeet pulled Tania in and she joined the frenzy. The uncles and aunties retired, but the boys and girls went on, uninterrupted, till the early hours of the morning.

In bed, finally, at three in the morning, she marveled at the boisterous, charged up atmosphere of the place, the never-ending carnival that was Nandita bua's home.

On her last day in Ludhiana, as Tania sat alone in the living room, she thought about how she would narrate these last few days to Mom. The birthday party, Pinky aunty, Pari messing her hair every ten minutes, Harmeet saying Dad was a postman. She smiled to herself.

Her thoughts drifted to the message on Dad's phone. It had been imprinted in her mind. *Miss you. Can't wait to see you tomorrow.* She had recognized the name of the sender. A colleague from his office.

She didn't know why she hadn't told Mom. She should. It was her right to know.

"*Taste kar*. Is the salt okay?" Nandita bua walked in with a bowl of rajma. "A penny for your thoughts."

"Nothing, bua. Bas thinking about going home tomorrow. I had so much fun. Thank you for having us."

"*Pagal*. You don't thank bua. You're always welcome here." Nandita hugged her.

It was then the brave face she had put up the entire time since Bali gave way, and she cried.

Nandita looked puzzled. "Arey, what happened?"

Tania put her head on bua's shoulder and wept bitterly.

Yes Boss

Sameer's brows narrowed in a frown as he dug out the newspaper cutting left in his in-box amongst piles of reports and mail. The quarterly results had been published and *his* name appeared as the signatory for management. He had signed off only on the provisional statements. Ketan had the responsibility for the final ones.

What was going on? First, Biochem figures get included in the Stonewell financial statements and then they get published, not in Ketan's name but in my name.

With the public issue coming up, it could be seen as a deliberate move to overstate profits. *How could a company like Stonewell indulge in an act so unethical?* There had to be another explanation. He needed to straighten it out with Ketan.

He called Ritu.

"Hey," she said softly.

"Hey. Is Ketan free?"

"Aww, you didn't call for me?" she drawled, feigning disappointment.

"Please. It's urgent. I need to talk to him." His fingers drummed the table.

"He's in a meeting," she said. "I'm looking at his calendar and… his day is full. He's free only at six."

"Can you please pencil me in?"

"Sure. Is there anything else I can do for you?" She switched to her official voice. Someone must be near; he mentally thanked whoever that was. He wasn't feeling up to frivolous love chatter right then.

After his return from Bali, they had a major row over her SMS. He had broken up with her. "I can't take the guilt anymore."

It hadn't lasted though. Within a week, they were back together.

His mind kept going back to the quarterly reports. He needed some advice. *Anand?*

"Haan, Sameer," Anand said, as he picked up the phone, "I'm in a meeting… can I call you back in ten minutes?"

Always busy.

He didn't have too many friends he could share his predicament with. "It's urgent yaar. I *have* to talk to you."

"I'll call you in ten minutes."

Anand called exactly ten minutes later. "Is everything okay?"

"Not really, yaar." His hand drew two tiny ovals on the note pad.

After he had recounted the piece about the quarterly financial statements, Anand's first reaction was predictable. "You are fucked." He continued. "Why the hell did you sign the statements? Man, that's the kind of thing they teach you in elementary school…"

"It was stupid. *Par ho gaya yaar.* The question is what do I do now?" The tiny ovals on the note pad were now enclosed in a big circle, eyes on a face.

"Well… to start with, talk to Ketan. He's always liked you. And Stonewell is not a rogue company."

"I want to get out of this cesspool, yaar. Talk to your contacts; see if they can find me an interesting position someplace else." The nose on the face was beaky and big.

"I'll try, man. But times are bad. Most of us are glad to be holding on to the jobs we have. You should've moved out years ago, when most of us left. But you had this grand ambition of being Stonewell's

CFO. Anyway, not important right now. Focus on this quarterlies shit. Tell me how it goes with Ketan."

He felt better having talked to Anand. He had voiced Sameer's own thoughts. *Stonewell isn't a rogue company.*

At six, he walked the short distance to Ketan's room. Ritu winked at him as he passed her desk.

Ketan sat behind his gleaming teak desk, looking intently at his desktop screen. Except for the gold pen stand and a family picture, the table was bare. *How did he keep his desk so clean?* Ketan wore a crisp white shirt and a red and black tie; the jacket of his grey suit hung behind his chair. Clipped french beard, salt-pepper hair neatly combed, lean body, Ketan exuded power. A man in control of his destiny.

"Sameer!" Ketan welcomed him, the voice of a top executive, not betraying the displeasure at the interruption. "How're you?"

Sameer wasn't sure where to sit – on the chairs in front of Ketan's desk or the sofa in the sitting area. So he stood, holding on to one of the chairs instead. "It's about the quarterly financial statements. I was surprised to see the reports published in my name. I mean… generally it's the CFO who signs off on the report." He decided to park himself on the chair he held.

Ketan peered at him and then broke into a smile. "Are you complaining we've given you an important role?"

"No, I didn't mean that," he said. "But I had signed off on provisional statements—"

"Nitin and I were both away from office at the time. So we decided to rely on your judgment and the signing off was delegated to you. Is that a problem?"

"No…no, that's not a problem. But I was told to include Biochem figures in the quarterly reports, and as you know, Biochem was not a subsidiary as on March 31."

"*Told to?*" Ketan's tone was sharp. "By whom?"

"My team – Kartik – he confirmed you had approved it…though."

"Well well…Sameer," Ketan wheeled his chair back, his fingers steepled in front of him. "This is interesting. Hmm… so let's see if I got that right. You signed inaccurate financial statements, violating Company law, SEBI regulations because Kartik *told* you to? That doesn't sound very responsible. You know Company law better than anyone; I've heard you quote chapter and verse."

Sameer felt sick in the pit of his stomach.

Ketan leant back in his chair. "I'm the CFO of the company. I don't have time for details. I leave it to my managers, who are smart and competent to take these calls." He paused, for effect, "Managers like you."

"I signed those statements believing the orders came from you. I left a note for you, Srini and the Board explaining the entire situation."

Ketan had the look of a pugilist on his face. Readying for the fight to begin. "Do you have a copy of that note?"

"No, I…"

Ketan's tense body relaxed, but he continued to stare at Sameer. "I suggest you be more careful in what you sign. That's what the company expects from a senior manager."

They were interrupted by a knock. Gopu, the coffee boy. Sameer watched as he poured the coffee into the gold-rimmed white porcelain cups. He felt nauseous.

"I guess there has been a snafu then. The question is what do we do about it now?" Sameer asked, after Gopu left.

Ketan took a long sip of the coffee. "For your sake, Sameer, let's hope the snafu, as you call it, is not discovered."

"But there is a public issue scheduled next month. There could be major repercussions if this is reported…"

"Precisely why it's important it's not discovered. It would be hard for me to defend you if it was."

Sameer felt heat radiating from his face and neck. He couldn't believe this was happening.

There was a lull in the conversation. Ketan was daring him to say more. He realized he couldn't. Anand was right. He was fucked.

"Anything else, Sameer?"

There was nothing to be said. This was a man whose professional excellence he had admired, who he considered his mentor. If he was out to get him, what was there to say?

Ketan was his top management self again, the charm back in his voice. "Don't worry too much. People have short memories. Once the public issue is over, I'm sure we'll figure out a way to fix it."

Ketan offered his hand and smiled. "Let's go for a drink when all this hoopla about the public issue is over. Talk about the old times."

The meeting was over.

Aware of Ritu's eyes on him, as he walked out of Ketan's room, Sameer didn't look up. He wanted to be alone.

Entering his room, he shut the door behind him. He considered his options. Not many. None attractive. Confronting Kartik wouldn't help; he could deny his involvement and there wasn't any evidence to the contrary. Sameer could quit and go public – disclosing the company had cheated on its quarterly results. But then his neck would be the first in line. He had signed the reports. He could report to the *goras* in London or Srini, the CEO here. But it was his word against Ketan's. Who were they going to believe – the CFO of the company or the Assistant Financial Controller who had signed off on those statements? Of course, he could stay quiet. That would be in line with what he usually did. Nothing.

But what if this got out?

He heard the click of the door knob. Ritu.

"What's wrong?" she asked, stepping inside his room and closing the door behind her. She stood right next to him. He could smell the faint fragrance of her perfume. She looked alluring in the pale pink sari with the grey paisleys. He felt an urge to hold her. To escape from the mess he had got himself into. He put his arms around her waist and pulled her closer to him.

"Not here," she whispered.

He brushed his face on her flat stomach, hiding himself.

She was getting turned on. Her fingers combed through his hair as she whispered, "What do you want?"

He got up from his chair and held her from behind. He loved the back of her neck; vulnerable and pure. He kissed the light brown mole that was a shade darker than her skin and rubbed himself on her hips. "You."

"Someone could come in," she said. But there was no conviction in her voice.

His hand was inside her blouse, under her bra, massaging her bare breast. He bent down and gathered up her sari, baring her legs. With her free hand, she held up her bunched sari, letting him run his hand over her legs and between. He could feel her arousal, the quickening of her breath. She let go of her hand on the sari and turned around and unzipped him as they kissed passionately.

The lights went off. It was seven. The energy saving lights were designed to automatically switch off at that time. They were entwined in each other's arms in the darkness.

He broke away and sat on a chair, drawing her with him. She smiled as she looked in his eyes. She bunched up the sari above her hips, peeled the panties off her legs, and lowered herself on him. In that half state of undress, he was inside her, feeling the familiar warmth.

They didn't hear the door because there was no knock. There was no knock because the room had been dark, and Ashok had presumed no one was in.

The three of them froze for an instant when Ashok stepped in and the motion sensor switched the lights back on. And then, there was a flurry of action. Ritu getting off him, Sameer scrambling to cover his nakedness, and Ashok realizing what he had stumbled upon, walking out of the room and shutting the door behind him.

Black

Kavita woke up with a smile on her face. The dream was still fresh in her mind. She had been in her childhood home with her mother. She fussed over Kavita. Made her *kheer*, took her to a circus, and bought her clothes. Then her mother told her to go back to Tania and Pari. She was in a bus going to Delhi to meet them, but it broke down and she was back with her mother again.

She remembered a line of Janos Arany. *'In dreams and in love, there are no impossibilities.'*

It was nice to see her mother in the dream.

After her mother's death, for some time she had dreamt of her almost every day. The dreams gradually declined and then stopped altogether. She felt a little guilty, as if ceasing to dream of her was the same as ceasing to remember her. She *wanted* to dream of her. She tried many things – looking at her picture, thinking of an anecdote, reading her letters, but nothing helped. She realized then that you couldn't will your dreams.

She heard Sameer in the shower. He had been tense the last few days. Kavita wished he would talk with her. Perhaps she could put things in perspective; he worried over little things.

After Sameer and the kids left, the house was quiet again. Feeling nostalgic about her mother, she took out the photo album her father had given her after her mother's death. Thick black pages, interspersed with sheer leaves. The photographs at the beginning were black and white. The first was a wedding photograph of her parents. You could barely see their faces. Her mother's *ghoonghat* revealing a bit of her chin, her father's *sehra* parted a little to reveal his grin.

The second picture was taken a few days after their marriage. Her father sat on a carved chair, resplendent in a three-piece suit, his waxed moustache rolled into fine tips at the ends. Her mother stood beside him, looking at the camera in a look of half hope, half despair. At the time of the picture, a few days after the wedding, had she figured out that behind his stern exterior, her husband was a softie? A poet.

She looked at her mother's face. There was a subtle beauty about her. Growing up, she had never been able to trace any resemblance with her. And now with the girls too, neither Tania nor Pari looked like Kavita. Tania had a bit of Sameer in her and Pari's look was entirely her own. *Something to do with the genes of her family; the daughters grew up looking unlike their mothers.* There were a few more pictures of theirs before Kavita's began. The album was really about her, their much pampered only child. Each picture of hers had a story associated with it. Some, she remembered well, some vaguely.

There she was, in a Himachali costume, the picture taken on a vacation in Shimla. She must have been five. She had dutifully struck the pose the photographer demanded of her, an earthen pitcher held at the waist, a far off look in her eyes, the dupatta held coyly over her cheek.

She flicked another page. Four-year-old Kavita sat on a small chair and table on the porch of their home in Chandigarh. The picture had been taken when her best friend Rani and she were playing cards.

The lonely child that she was, she had yearned for company before she found Rani. She played with her for hours. The unique thing about Rani, however, was that she didn't really exist, except in her imagination. In the photo, two hands had been dealt, for Rani and her. Her father had made sure he captured it in the photograph. Rani's presence had been a major source of amusement for him.

She had made her so real that she even complained about Rani to her mother.

"She used a bad word."

"She won't talk to me today."

"She cheats at Ludo."

Her mother played along as she did the housework. It was when Kavita went to school and made flesh and blood friends that she let Rani slip away from her.

One album – many remembrances. Moments, memories, dreams. Her treasure.

In the evening, Kavita sat on the balcony, enjoying the post-rain breeze. The fragrance of wet earth hung in the air. The sky was a painting of gray and orange brushstrokes. Monsoon was in full swing and she loved this time of the year. The darkening of the skies in the middle of the day, the sudden downpours, the respite from heat.

The breeze moved the strands of the palm fronds individually, like invisible fingers playing on a piano. A sparrow landed near the jasmine bush and pranced around. It moved its head in tiny, jerky moments. The wind blew droplets from jasmine leaves to the ground in a tiny shower. Little white buds had begun to appear on the shrub.

She closed her eyes to enjoy the cool breeze on her face.

"Kavita ji, lovely weather *na*?" Payal called out from her balcony next door. She opened her eyes and nodded in agreement. Payal looked elegant in her grapefruit-pink churidar and matching heels.

"I made Jackfruit pakoras. Roasted, not fried. Very healthy. I'll send you some. They'll be great with some *garam garam chai*."

She didn't have the heart to tell Payal that the idea of roasted jackfruit pakoras didn't sound too appetizing. The park in front of their house was at its greenest. The trees looked washed of their dust and grime, the grass browned by summer heat was growing back, the hedges had gotten their colour back. Monsoon in Delhi had its own problems – flooding, traffic jams, power outages – but she and the park both enjoyed the weather.

She had been re-reading Jhumpa Lahiri's *The Namesake*. She marveled at the writer's ability to tug at hearts without being melodramatic. She wished she could write like her. That had been her one big dream. To be a novelist.

She started twice. First, in Chandigarh when she was in college, and then again when Tania begun school and she found herself with time on her hands. The second time, she had gone on to four chapters. A romance between a soldier and a peasant girl set in Punjab. She had shown the draft to Pallavi, the editor of *Reflections* – the magazine she contributed poetry to – and she had liked it. Pallavi encouraged Kavita to continue. Kavita wrote one more chapter and then lost steam. The words on the paper sounded artificial, nowhere close to what she wanted to say.

Maybe she should have persisted. She may have had a career. Forty-two, and there wasn't much she could claim in terms of accomplishments. Women her age ran business empires, managed conglomerates.

She heard footsteps behind her and then Pari's soft arms were wrapped around her neck from behind. She pressed her cheek on Pari's arm. "You didn't tell me about school today."

Pari didn't need a second invitation. She let go of her and sat down cross-legged on the chair beside her. "You didn't even ask about the field trip. You always forget."

"*Always*?"

Pari laughed. "We went to an insectarium today."

"Eww."

"Mom, insects are cool! Butterflies are insects too. They're not eww." Pari's arms flapped in the air like a butterfly in flight.

Kavita had to admit they were not.

"You know, some butterflies use their front legs to clean their eyes," Pari said.

"Really? I never thought of butterflies with eyes and legs… just wings with amazing colours and patterns."

"And you know what?" Pari asked. In her excitement, she had climbed on her lap. She was no longer small, but climbed laps like she was still a baby. "I had the world's longest insect on my arm. It's called stick insect. Looks just like a twig."

"Didn't it scare you?"

"Nope." She shook her head, enjoying her mother's unease. "It even moved a bit." She moved her two fingers on Kavita's arm.

"Eww…." She had copied saying 'eww' from Pari. It was interesting how Pari's words became hers, even when Pari herself moved on.

She cupped her cheeks and kissed her forehead. "You seem to have fun all the time, lucky ducky."

Pari buried her face in Kavita's bosom and wrapped her arms around her.

"Where's Tania?" Kavita asked.

"New York!" Pari replied in a muffled voice and then lifted her head. "Where else but her room?"

"Ask her to come and sit with us. The weather is nice."

Pari raised her head. "Why? Are you bored with me?"

She smiled. "No darling. How can I ever be bored of you? You're the biggest source of entertainment in my life."

Tania was at the threshold of the balcony a little later and shouted from there, "You called?"

"Come, get some fresh air."

"Fresh air? Delhi is one of the most polluted cities in the world."

"Not after it rains."

Pari was back at her old spot, lying down supine on her lap.

"I have a test tomorrow," Tania said.

"Why don't you bring your books here?"

"Ma, can't study here with all that noise."

"Achha, sit with me for a while… *baad mein padh lena.*"

Tania came out to the balcony and sat down on the chair beside her.

"Is something wrong? You've been quiet," Kavita asked, looking at Tania.

"Not at Bua's place. She talked all the time," Pari said.

"Shut up, loser!" Tania was quick to silence her. Pari buried her face back in her mother's lap.

"There's nothing, Ma," Tania said.

She took Tania's hand into hers. She noticed the long nails and blue nail polish, a woman's hand practically. "Baby, you know you can tell me anything."

She sensed a hesitation in Tania as if she was deciding if she should. And then the decision was made. "There's nothing. I should go."

She let go of her hand and saw her walking back inside. She would talk when she was ready. She needed a little time. And a little persuasion.

"She's *always* mad." Pari's head was up again.

"You know why?"

"Because, she is a teenager." Pari made the sign of inverted commas with her hands. They laughed as Kavita hugged her.

"Pari! Milk," Ammaji called from inside.

She slid off Kavita, shaking her head. "*Yeh Ammaji na.* She never forgets."

Maybe she hadn't too badly, after all. She had raised two loving kids and she enjoyed their company.

She sipped the tea Ammaji had left by her side, savoring its milky cardamom taste. Reaching for the book, her hand touched another paper and she picked it up. The poem she had started months ago, *A few moments more*. She had forgotten all about it. She should finish it. But not right then. She was enjoying her reading. She folded the paper, inserted it in the book, and started reading again.

She first felt a discomfort in her chest, right in the middle, like a pressure, a squeezing. And then it went away. Moments later, she felt it again, a little more this time.

It was only a few minutes later, when she felt a shortness of breath, as if the air around her had been sucked away, that the alarm bell went off in her mind. She panicked, as another wave of pain hit her. This time it wasn't mere discomfort. It was pain. It was as if someone sat on her chest, squeezing her insides hard.

She tried getting up. Her head spun; the balcony, the trees, the sky above, in a swift swirl, like some crazy upside-down ride. She fell back in the chair, her breath coming in violent fits – uneven, sharp. She shouted for Ammaji. The pain had spread to her arms and shoulders. Her shirt stuck to her back as she felt a cold sweat breaking out. Fear gripped her. She knew it was a heart attack.

By the time Ammaji heard her muffled cries and came rushing outside, the children at her heels, her senses had dimmed. She could see Ammaji wringing her hands in despair, Tania frantically punching numbers on her phone, Pari crying – but it was as if she watched them from a distance. She wanted to reach out and hug the girls, to tell them not to worry, that she was going to be fine. It was then that her world went black.

Race

It started raining as they dashed into the car to take Mom to the hospital. The streets were saturated already and some of them flooded. The traffic slowed and then halted near Sheikh Sarai. Frantic, Tania dialled Dad's mobile again. No answer. At home, she had called his office number, to be told he hadn't come in that day. *Where the hell was he? Why didn't he pick up?*

She hadn't known where to take Mom. It was Dayal who suggested Max Hospital in Saket. Caught in the middle of the traffic jam, she thought of Sanjeevani nursing home, two blocks from their house. They could have called for an ambulance; maybe the traffic would have made way for it. They were stuck now. There was no going back.

She jumped out of the car, the water lapping at her ankles, madly waving at the circuitous lines of immobile vehicles blocking their way. She ran through the traffic, her clothes wet, searching for a way out of the jam. People stared at her.

The window of a white Maruti Esteem unrolled. A balding middle-aged man with rimless glasses called out to her, "What's wrong, beta?" He had a kind face that looked vaguely familiar.

She was hysterical in her response. *Mother. Sick. Hospital. Rain. Traffic.*

The man dialled a number on her cell and urged her to go back to her car. "Don't worry. Everything will be fine."

Through the rain pelting on the car window, she could see her mother was still unconscious. Ammaji rubbed her Mom's feet vigorously, as if warm feet were going to save her life. Pari was crying and signaled her to come back inside the car. She did but jumped out again when the traffic refused to move and slipped on the wet leaves on the pavement. She held back her tears, unwilling to give up hope.

She heard the sound of the siren before she saw the ambulance. As the para-medical staff moved her Mom, she glanced, in gratitude, towards the man in white Maruti Esteem. He waved and wished her luck.

When they reached the hospital, the ward boys wheeled her Mom into Emergency. She plopped down in a chair, relieved. They were in good hands. It was also when her father finally called back. Things were falling in place.

Pari's crying was beginning to annoy her. She wanted to shush her, to tell her it was bad luck to shed tears. But her attention was riveted to the door to the emergency room. A doctor, still in his operation theatre scrubs, walked briskly towards it. He looked to be her Dad's age. A little stoop, a kind but tired face. When he looked in their direction, she stood up.

"Please," she said, folding her hands, no other words coming out of her mouth. He patted her hands and hurried in.

She hugged a still sobbing Pari. "She's going to be fine."

There was a blur of activity. Each time someone stepped out of the emergency room, she stood up, heart in mouth. The air conditioning in the hospital felt cold on her wet clothes and her head thrummed with white noise, like someone had left a hundred radios running inside. They would talk about this one day – Mom and her. How scared Tania had been. She would ensure that her Mom exercised and dieted; she couldn't take chances with her health.

She stood up again when the doctor in scrubs came out of the emergency room, looking even more tired than before.

He approached them and asked her gently, "Is your Dad here?"

"He's on his way, doctor. He should be here any minute," she replied, her voice tight with fear.

He hesitated. "We'll wait for him."

When he started to walk away, she felt sick; an unknown fear gnawed at her. She ran out to catch up with him. "Is my Mom alright? If you need anything – blood or something – I… I can help."

He put his arm around her shoulder and sat her on a chair close to where they stood. There was a long pause.

"I'm sorry."

"What?" She stood up. The radios inside her head were louder.

"I'm very sorry. Your mother… is no more. She was brought dead. We tried to revive her, but…"

"Brought dead?" The words tumbled out of her mouth. It seemed unreal, a scene out of a TV show or something.

There was a strange tingling in her scalp. A current ran through the base of her spine. The doctor's image became hazy. She thought her legs would buckle, but she continued to stand even though nothing supported her.

How easily did he say it? How objectively. Like it was all a make-believe kids' game where her mother was playing dead and he was pretending to be a doctor with a toy stethoscope around his neck.

She wrenched away from the man, and ran towards the emergency room to see her mother. *It couldn't be. How could she die? She was forty-two. People don't die at that age. They die after they have grandchildren and great grandchildren.*

Two ward boys, emerging from inside, held her back. She screamed and jostled with them, called them morons and gold diggers. She *had* to see her mother. They *had* to let her see her mother.

She saw her father rushing into the hospital, just before she was taken inside for sedation.

"You killed her!" She shouted at the top of her voice, pointing a finger at him, and turning every head in their direction, "*You killed her!*"

Tania sat next to Nandita bua amidst the neighbouring women surrounding them. The living room was no longer how her mother had decorated it. Sofa chairs and the glass topped coffee table were replaced by sheets laid out on the carpet.

At the other end of the room, where the men sat, her father and Daadu folded their hands in response to a neighbour who had gotten up to leave. She hated this endless procession of visitors. People coming in, folding their hands, sitting down and commiserating.

"I'm so sorry."

"She was such a good woman."

"You have to be brave."

A charade. They were belittling her loss, her unbearable ache, by meaningless words. She wished them gone. She wished to be alone with people who really cared. She wanted to complain to Mom. *This is what happened when you died.*

Her father sat on the floor, dressed in a white kurta pajama. She hadn't spoken with him since the hospital. She couldn't bear to. *Where was he when Mom was dying?*

Pari had left her side some time ago and Tania got up to look for her. Pari wasn't in her room. Ammaji hadn't seen her either. She entered Mom's bedroom to find Pari sprawled on the bed, on her stomach. Tania sat beside her and caressed her hair.

Pari said looking at her, "I came here looking for her. I… forgot she was dead."

She searched Tania's face. "Did it happen to you too?"

Tania nodded, her hand on Pari's cheek.

"I didn't find her here. But in this room, in this bed, on these sheets, I can smell her. It's almost like she's here... like she'll be here any minute."

They cried, hugging each other.

"You know what I regret the most?" Tania said, her voice breaking, "I didn't spend time with her yesterday. I wish I had told her how much I loved her."

"She knew."

They lay talking a long time till Tania could feel the level breathing of her sister's little body. She was asleep. At least a few moments of peace for her. Perhaps she will have a pleasant dream, see Mom.

Hum Tum Aur Ghost

It all started with the bottle of hand lotion. Sameer's hands felt rough and he reached for it on the table on Kavita's side of the bed. Past the photo frame of the monkey in grass skirt with maracas in hand, that held Tania's picture with 'Happy Mother's Day' written at the base. In the last two days, he had been caught in the the numbing world of activities – things that had to be done – paper work, cremation, condolers. As he rubbed the lotion on his hands, Kavita quietly filled the room. The shock was immediate. A punch in the gut.

He remembered the silent dance of her hands applying the lotion. Playing to the music of her bangles. Left on right, right on left, side by side. The scent of jasmine.

The other articles in the room joined in the torment. The bronze chappal that peeked out of her closet, half in, half out. The first thing he had seen on entering the hospital room. The tiny marble box on the dresser with the red and blue carving they had bought together in an Agra bazaar. The water colour landscape above the TV, the only remnant of her brief fling with painting. The smudges on the mountain, her failed experimentation with a lighter colour. Her pillow that still bore the imprint of her head.

He curled into himself, defending against their onslaught, under the sheets, knees to the chest. *Was this grief?* It hurt. It immobilized him.

Knocking on the door. Knuckles rapping against the wood.

Go away. Leave me alone with Kavita's ghost.

The knocking continued. In a voice that faintly resembled his, he asked to be left alone.

His father's voice. Urgency in it. He tried to get up. The simple process of taking a step takes two hundred and twenty muscles to work together. His legs finally making it to the door. His father. His mother and Pari behind him. Expressions ranging from concern to fear.

He has to be strong, his father told him.

He knew. *Is it asking too much to spend some time alone with my wife's ghost?*

Two hundred and twenty muscles coordinated unwillingly again to take him back to bed.

He didn't know what hurt him more. The loss or the remorse. He was in no position to analyze; together they were a deadly combination. *The retribution is disproportionate to my crimes. Death is an unjust punishment. When did Kavita get so vindictive?*

He could count on fingers the number of fights they had in all these years. The time she insisted he stayed the night at her parents' even though her father wouldn't talk to him. Lying sleepless in the room of her childhood, her photographs pasted all over the walls, he had fumed, called her a wimp.

Or the time returning from a party, he had crashed the car in the garage of their own home. Both of them were unhurt, but the front of the car had suffered damage.

Or over Pari's name. Pratishtha was too heavy weight for him. But she insisted it was the meaning of the word that mattere. Honour.

She won in the end, mostly.

There was not even the comfort of afterlife to make things better. He didn't believe. Nor did Kavita.

He lay there a long time. Kavita's ghost flitted in and out.

When he got up, it was dark outside. Except for the lone bulb in the hallway, the lights were out.

He walked out to the balcony, taking in the mossy, damp air. The trees in the park were dark monsters, alert and watchful.

I must seek forgiveness. I must atone.

Inspector Eagle

Sameer sat cross-legged on the floor, receiving condolences from a neighbour when Ammaji told him about the policemen waiting outside. He rose and walked out, conscious of all eyes following him. The sitting area, generally bare, looked like a warehouse, crammed with furniture removed from the living room to make space for the mourners. Two uniformed men sat on the sofa that was covered in a sheet.

"Sorry, sir ji, we're disturbing you at a time like this. We're very sorry for your loss," the younger looking man said, rising to shake Sameer's hand. He introduced himself as Sub-Inspector Rajender Singh Rawat. He looked to be in his thirties; medium built, clipped moustache and a no-nonsense haircut. His eyes seemed to be everywhere, evaluating everything, everyone. The other guy was introduced as Constable Singh. A bumpy nose – Owen Wilson style – and a serious pot belly.

Rawat explained their presence, "Sir ji, there has been a complaint and we've come for an enquiry. I hope you don't mind if we ask you a few questions."

"Complaint?"

"Haanji. If this is not a good time…"

Sameer was curious. "It's fine. We can talk now."

114

"Your name?" Rawat asked.

As Sameer answered, Singh opened up a file that he held in his hand like a folded newspaper. It held one yellowing sheet of paper. Reaching into his shirt pocket, he pulled out a much-chewed pen and began to write.

"Address? You live in this house, sir?" Rawat asked again.

"Of course. Can you please tell me what the complaint is?"

"*Likh bhai,* Singh, 60, Panchsheel Enclave." Rawat ignored Sameer and nodded at the constable, who wrote diligently.

Keshav was leaving and Sameer folded his hands in response. Through his thick glasses, Keshav glanced at Rawat and Singh, as he shut the door behind him.

Rawat continued, "When did this happen, this *haadsa,* this incident?"

Sameer looked at Rawat, surprised. "Haadsa? My wife died on August 28 – three days ago. Of a heart attack." There was no air-conditioning in the sitting room and it felt muggy.

Sameer had a deep disdain for police – one of the most corrupt institutions in the country. Three years ago, there had been a burglary in their home. The thieves had broken into the house through the back door while they were away on a vacation. They had made away with a few pieces of jewellery and some cash. Filing an FIR had been more harrowing an experience than the theft itself. Overt demands for bribe and then reverse questioning of Sameer and Kavita when they refused to give in to their solicitation.

Ammaji put two steaming cups of milky tea on the table. Singh picked up his, blew on it and took a careful sip. Then rested his cup on his belly. The sticky sweet smell made Sameer's stomach churn. The outside door opened again and a woman he recognized as a neighbour but didn't quite know folded her hands to him. She took off her chappals, covered her head with her dupatta, and went in the living room to sit with the women.

There were a couple of more inane questions and he managed to answer them without losing his cool. It was then that Tania passed them on her way to the living room. Rawat's eyes followed her till she was out of his sight. "Is that your daughter?"

"Yes."

"Can we talk to her?" Rawat leaned forward.

"No," he said. "I don't think it'd be appropriate. She's a minor and has gone through too much already. Besides, you still haven't told me what the complaint is and what does it have to do with her."

"How old is she, sir ji?"

"Sixteen."

He hated the leer he detected on Rawat's face. "*Theek hai,* sir ji. This is enough. If required, we'll come back after a few days."

"Rawat sahib, why would you need to?" He asked, his anger at this needless invasion of his home, spilling out. "You've asked me a number of meaningless questions without telling me what the complaint is."

"We understand your loss, sir ji, but we're doing our duty—"

He snapped then. The façade of sanity he had been cultivating caved in and Rawat became the unlikely target of his unresolved emotions. How could Rawat claim to understand his loss when even Sameer was only beginning to comprehend the magnitude of what had hit him. "No, you don't understand my loss at all. I know your kind. If it's money you're after, tell me what you want, but please leave us alone." The words were unnecessarily harsh and he realized it as soon as he said them. But there they were, hanging in the air like a bad smell.

Rawat's face darkened. He ran his fingers over his moustache. "Sir ji, we've been civil to you. We've come to your house and asked a few questions respectfully. We could have called you to the police station and done the same with a lot less courtesy. We're not here for money. There has been a complaint and we *will* investigate it." He added, "And I *will* see you again."

Sameer's father ambled into the room. "Is there a problem?"

"No, Dad," Sameer replied, eyes on Rawat. "Rawat sahib had to make a routine enquiry. He's leaving."

"Namaste, sir." Rawat got up, folded his hands and bent a good thirty degrees from his waist in his father's direction, a picture of civility. "Yes, we're leaving." Turning to Sameer, he said, "We'll meet again."

"One last question." It was Singh speaking for the first time, pen poised on the paper, "Where were you at the time of the death?"

"In my office."

It was the day after Rawat's unwelcome intrusion. There was a let up in the visits of condolers. Sameer sat at his desk in the bedroom, checking his e-mails. More to distract himself than to get anything useful accomplished. Pari came in and hugged him from behind.

He patted her hand. "Did you have lunch?"

She nodded.

He turned and winked at her. "I want ice cream."

Nirula's was two blocks away. They walked together, her hand in his. A hawker announced to the world he sold genuine Kashmiri hand-woven shawls. There was the smell of *bhutta* being roasted on coals. A queue had formed at the big blue drop of Mother Dairy. People talked, complained, fought, ate, drank. The normalcy was reassuring in a way. That outside 60, Panchsheel Park, life went on.

"*Teri wohi?* Regular?" He asked her when they reached Nirula's.

"I don't want any."

"*Kha le na.*"

"One strawberry, one Delhi delight. Both cones," he said to the guy with braces at the cash counter.

They were the only customers in the restaurant. They sat close to the window, silently licking their ice creams. Across the street, amongst the neat pyramids of apples and oranges, a young couple shared a glass of juice. The afternoon traffic trickled.

There was blankness in her eyes that pained him. He wished he could say words to make her feel better. "What are you thinking?"

She shook her head, as a drop of melting ice-cream dripped on to her tank top.

"I know what you're thinking," he said. "You're thinking Dad's ice cream looks better than mine."

Despite herself, she smiled, cleaning herself with a napkin.

"You can always ask me for a lick."

"Dad!"

He touched the half-dimple formed on her cheek. "We should do this every week. The ice cream is refreshing and you are fantastic company."

She laughed.

They were almost done, when she spoke, "Dad?"

"Hmm?"

"I love you."

A lump lodged itself in the middle of his throat. "I love you too."

Kama Sutra

If only he had picked up the phone.

Ritu had slowed down when the phone rang for the first time. But he let it ring. She smiled at him, as he closed his eyes to enjoy the sensations she was causing him. He wanted the release that Ashok's unexpected interruption had denied him the day before. His fingers played with her nipples, as he moved beneath her, wanting her to rush. The phone rang again and he stretched his arm to switch it off. She increased the pace again, moving up and down on him, as he lay with eyes closed and his hands on her breasts, egging her on silently. She stopped when she felt him getting there, but he couldn't wait. He moved her off him. Her long legs on his shoulders, he plunged deep into her. Hard, deep strokes. The way she loved them. They came about the same time. It was intense for both, as they held each other tight, lips on lips, limbs on limbs.

They lay quietly, in each other's arms, the phone forgotten. They hadn't gone to the office that day; they knew that ridicule and shame awaited them there. By then, Ashok must have told everyone.

He drifted off to sleep.

It was when he woke up that he saw the seventeen missed calls from Tania.

Run

Ritu woke up to the beep of the phone. Rain drops fell gently against the window panes. The sound of pigeons' muted cooing filtered in as they sheltered under the awning of her window. It was dark outside. She looked at her bedside clock and was surprised. Nine at night. She had slept through the evening and hadn't even picked Aayush up from her parents' place.

She reached for her cell-phone to call her parents and then remembered that it was the sound of the phone that had woken her. She sat upright with a jolt as she read Sameer's message.

Earlier in the evening, when Sameer left in haste, she had a feeling it was serious. Hospitalization could mean anything – high fever, dengue, food poisoning. Grave enough to be taken to hospital, but not necessarily life-threatening. But something told her this was life and death serious.

A range of emotions gripped her. Sadness. Guilt. Fear.

She didn't know much about Kavita. Slivers of information gathered in passing. Sameer didn't say much and she hadn't asked. It worked for her – not conjuring the reality of Kavita in her fantasy world. However, in that moment, she wanted to know. What was she like? What were her dreams? What did she die thinking? She felt a surge of self-reproach rise within her.

Home wrecker. Killer. She lay curled up in the dark, listening to the rain pelting the windows.

The next morning, though her mind was still tormented by self-loathing, Ritu steeled herself to go to the office. The news of Kavita's death must have reached them too. Blame, condemnation, humiliation – whatever it was – she would have to deal with it.

She wore a white chiffon sari with black polka dots. Her eyes looked a little puffy and she applied some mascara.

As soon as she stepped inside the glass doors of the office, she saw Neena talking to Mitali, the receptionist. An arrangement of pink roses and white gladiolas sat on the reception desk. They stopped talking and looked at her.

Here it comes.

"Did you hear?" Neena asked.

"What?" She asked, her throat dry, fidgeting with the pallu of her sari.

"Sameer's wife passed away," Neena said, searching her face. "You didn't know?"

"No." She surprised herself with how easily she lied.

Neena seemed pleased her thunder hadn't been stolen.

So the news about me and Sameer hasn't reached Neena. But then, she was called the zombie for a reason.

Ritu smiled at Shalini and Kumar as she entered her cubicle; they were her neighbours. Shalini stood up from her seat and looked at her with her elbows resting on top of the wooden partition. Shalini was young, in her mid-twenties, and was new in the office.

"You heard?" Shalini asked.

"Neena told me."

"Did you know her?"

"Not really. I saw her a few times at office parties…" *But I knew the husband intimately. In fact, he was making love to me at my house when she died.*

Without pausing the punching on his keyboard, Kumar piped in, a thick Keralite accent in his tone, "Heart attacks so *cammon thhese* days. It is *aall* lifestyle. Sitting all day and eating. Nothing *ellse. Tcah!* "

As the day progressed, it became clear no one knew about her and Sameer.

It was in the late afternoon she saw Ashok for the first time. Over the last few years, Ashok's beard had grown in direct proportion to the loss at the top of his head. He deposited a sheaf of papers in her inbox and cleared her outbox. Instead of the leer she had expected on his face, Ashok made a conscious attempt not to look at her, his eyes downcast. He was about to leave, when she stopped him. "Ashok ji?"

"Yes, madam?" He was still looking at the papers, avoiding her eyes.

"Thank you."

"It's… alright, madam," he stammered and walked out.

She felt indebted to him, for his generosity of not humiliating Sameer and her.

Immediately afterwards, Ritu felt contrite, realizing her misplaced focus. Worrying about her own ignominy at a time a catastrophe had struck. *When did I become so self-centred?* She gave a silent prayer for forgiveness.

It was Kavita's *chautha*. Most of the office staff was going. She didn't want to. The idea of being face to face with Sameer's family was intimidating. Looking in the mirror was hard enough. But everyone in the office knew Sameer and Ritu to be good friends and it would raise eyebrows if she didn't go.

In the evening, as she left the office for the ceremony, she remembered it was her turn to pick Aayush up from her parents' place that day. She decided to take him along; his presence would fortify her.

Aayush was quiet during the ride; his seatbelt-bound lanky body leaning on the far side. She let him be, too nervous herself. When the two of them reached the temple, the ceremony had started. The hall was filling up. At an elevated place in the front, a priest sat performing the pooja with Sameer, Tania, Pari and the rest of the family. Others were seated in two gender-segregated rows. She settled Aayush on the men's side and sat down cross-legged on the carpet in the women's section beside an elderly woman.

Her eyes went to the front. Tania sat next to her grandmother. She wore a white churidar kurta; her head covered with a black bordered dupatta. A comely young woman. Pari sat clinging to her father. Ritu felt like an impostor. She didn't belong, had no right to mourn. *Home wrecker. Killer.* She wished the rites would finish soon so she could leave, but the havan seemed to go on and on; the chanting of mantras, the offerings to the fire, the suffocating fragrance of the incense.

The first time Ritu heard the sound of stifled laughter from the men's side, breaking the monotony of the chanting, she thought it highly inappropriate. *Laughing at such an occasion.* After a short interval, there it was again, louder and clearer this time. She looked at Sameer and his daughters, glad they hadn't heard. When she heard it again, loud and uncontrolled, with a start she recognized it. She knew it even before she had looked in his direction.

Aayush was in a laughing fit. All eyes were on him; indignation on the faces of many. *Insulting the dead.*

Before she could get up to get hold of him and run out, Shalini had recognized him. "It's Aayush, Ritu's son," she said to no one in particular, looking for Ritu in the crowd, "He's autistic…."

Murmurs of understanding seemed to emanate from the crowd, as she heard the word *abnormal*. Her eyes stung.

The priest, a wizened, unhappy looking man, shouted, "Arrey, whose child is he? Please remove him from here!"

Ritu had seen Sameer glance at her and then look down. However, Tania's eyes remained on her as she struggled with Aayush. There was fire in those eyes. Her face burning, Ritu walked Aayush out of the hall. She felt hundreds of eyes prickling the back of her neck. She wished she hadn't come. She wished she hadn't brought Aayush. She wished Kavita was not dead and she wasn't inundated with guilt.

Aayush was still laughing as they reached the parking lot. She raised her hand and swung at his face hard. The laughter stopped. He stood, shocked, his hand on his cheek, unaware of why he had been hit.

She broke down and cried. She kissed and hugged him. "I'm sorry, Aayush."

Driving home, the image of Tania's eyes boring into her remained imprinted in her mind.

Sankat City

The morning after the Chautha, Rawat and his lackey showed up again. Led inside by Ammaji, they stood looking around the living room, restored to its original setting. The sofas, the paintings, the book cases were back to where they belonged. Sameer walked in, dressed in his office attire – a charcoal grey suit, white shirt and a light blue tie with a pattern of tiny golf clubs – irked at their unwelcome intrusion and yet a little apprehensive. "Morning Rawat sahib. What can I do for you?"

Rawat smiled, pleased at Sameer's displeasure. "Many things, sir ji. For a start, you can come to the police station with us."

"Why?" Sameer asked, his eyebrows joined together in a frown. He didn't even ask them to sit down.

"Because we're investigating if you had a role in your wife's death and..."

Sameer cut him short, his voice a decibel higher. "That's silly. My wife died of a heart attack. Are you saying I caused it?"

"Oh no, sir ji. *We* are not saying that. Your *daughter* said you killed her." Rawat smiled.

Sameer ignored the reference to Tania's outburst at the hospital. "I have a doctor's certificate to prove..."

"Please let me finish sir ji." Rawat held up his hand. "You lied to us. You were *not* in your office at the time of the death."

Sameer's tone softened. "Rawat sahib, please. You know very well my wife died of natural causes. Let's settle this peacefully."

Rawat's jaw was set. "Police Station, sir ji."

Sameer's shoulders drooped. He went to his bedroom where his father sat cross-legged on the bed, glasses perched on his nose, and his wooden book holder opened for *Geeta paath*. "Dad, I've to go to the police station."

His father pulled the saffron string that served as the bookmark and shut the *Geeta*. "I'll come too."

"No, you don't need to." He put a hand on his father's shoulder. "There's nothing to it. Routine procedure. I'll be back soon."

Grateful he didn't need to explain to the others – his mother and Nandita were still asleep with the girls in their room and his father-in-law was out for his morning walk – he trooped back to the policemen, the sound of his father's chanting following him.

When they got downstairs, he didn't see Rawat's motorcycle. "This way." He pointed at his Honda and pressed the unlock button on his key. The *tut-tut* sound rang out.

"Sir ji, we don't want to trouble you. Police station is not too far. Let's walk," Rawat said.

They want to walk me to the police station for everyone to see. Bastards.

Payal stood outside her gate, with a covered platter in her hand. She glanced at Rawat and Singh before turning to him. "Sameer ji, I had brought some *upma* for you."

"Thank you, Payal. Please give it to Ammaji. I'll have it for lunch," he assured her.

As they walked, Rawat said, "Sir ji, Singh was saying we should use these," he showed Sameer the handcuffs in his satchel, "but I told him I know Sameer sahib's kind. They're law abiding citizens."

Rawat and Singh walked on either side of him like they were escorting a criminal, attracting a number of curious glances. The office goers stepping out of their houses, the cleaning women sweeping the road, the drivers leaning against their cars waiting for their sahibs. If the objective of this parade was his humiliation, they had chosen the time well. He saw Kohli (he didn't know or ever wanted to know his first name), who lived on the same street, taking his car out from his porch. Usually, they acknowledged each other with a wave of the hand. But Kohli turned his head away and drove off. People were already pronouncing him guilty.

The police station was a small one floor building, painted in dark blue and red, the police colours, on the outside.

Sameer was escorted to a dark, dank office.

"Can I see the SHO?" He asked as soon as they went in.

Like he was going to be any different. But anyone but Rawat at this time.

"Of course sir ji. *Bade aadmi hain aap* – no one but the SHO sahib for you." In his own domain, Rawat seemed to be in even better humour.

Rawat sat down on his swivel chair behind the desk and signalled Sameer to sit on one of the chairs facing him. "Singh, *dekhna bhai,* if SHO sahib is in."

Sameer stood, hands in the pockets of his trousers, attempting to look nonchalant. Behind Rawat were steel bookshelves with hundreds of decaying files. The table was bare except for two large registers on one side. Singh retuned after a few minutes with a grin on his face. "Nahin sir, SHO sahib is on leave today. You're in-charge."

They were playing silly cat and mouse games with him.

"Oh! Sorry, Sameer sahib. Looks like I'm in-charge today. You'll have to do with me," he said in mock apology, pleased at his own joke.

They had timed this well.

Sameer felt suffocated in his jacket and tie. A ceiling fan rotated slowly over their heads, making more noise than air. He took his jacket off and sat down, ready for the charade to begin. Singh parked himself on the chair next to him. The room had a faint odour of urine. The peeling paint on the wall behind Rawat had left a pattern of a boat under a cloud.

He didn't know what they were after. They couldn't seriously think he had anything to do with Kavita's death. Maybe they thought he would pay more if they dragged him to the police station. *They were right.* He started thinking of the amount he should offer Rawat.

The place was strangely peaceful. They had run into two constables on his way in, who were reading different sections of the morning newspaper. They had gotten up, saluted Rawat and then gone right back to the daily. He didn't know Delhi was such a peaceful place. There wasn't any work for the police except harassing people who hadn't done any wrong.

Rawat struck a match to light the cigarette in his lips. The bright orange flame ebbed and then died. "Singh, *kuch khatirdari karo Sameer sahib ki,* he's our guest. Send someone for tea. Little sugar though. I am sure Sameer sahib doesn't take much. Sameer sahib, *samosey mangaoon?*" The chatter of a typewriter in the adjoining room made its way to them.

"No, thanks."

"Haanji, Sameer sahib," Rawat began, with an ironical emphasis on sahib, exhaling the smoke on the no-smoking sign on his desk. "Shall we start then? Why don't you begin by telling us how you committed the crime?"

Rawat was smiling. Sameer realized Rawat understood the absurdity of his accusation.

"Rawat sahib," he began calmly, "There hasn't been one. My wife died of natural causes. I have evidence…"

"*Toh sir ji,* you're not going to come clean. *Theek hai,*" he started again. "*Chaliye,* tell us where you were at the time of the crime?"

Crime!

Sameer drew close to the table, the expression on his face earnest. "Rawat sahib, tell me how much."

Mimicking Sameer, Rawat also leaned forward on the table. "Sameer sahib, do you even know what you're doing? You're trying to bribe a public servant. And this is the third time. One more time and no further questions. Lock-up."

Sameer looked at him. *Rawat meant it. It wasn't about money any longer.* He felt a terror of the unknown grip his heart. *What did Rawat want?*

"Where were you at the time of the crime?" Rawat asked again.

"But there was no—"

"Answer the question, sir ji." Rawat ran his fingers on his moustache.

"With a friend."

Singh asked, "Name of the friend?" The chewed up pen and the grey file cover had reappeared.

Sameer hesitated for a moment and saw anticipation in Rawat's eyes. They had figured there was something Sameer wanted to hide.

"Name of the friend, sir ji," Rawat prompted him. He looked at Sameer intently. The cigarette turned into ash between his fingers.

"Ritu. Ritu Mathur."

Rawat and Singh exchanged a look, like they had struck jackpot.

"Ah, I see! A lady friend?" Rawat said with a derisive grin on his face. "So you were with a lady friend when your wife…"

Sameer felt naked, exposing his life to the scrutiny of these men.

"And where does your lady friend live?" Singh asked.

"Rawat sahib. Please. Can we keep her out of this?"

Rawat bent across the table towards Sameer. "Keep her out? Sir ji, she's right in the middle. We'll need to talk to her to check your alibi."

He leaned back in his chair, as he grinned at him in satisfaction. "After all, we still don't know if you're telling the truth."

Singh asked again, "The address, sir?"

"120 B, Malviya Nagar." Stories of Sunil's violent ways ran in his mind. "Can I make one request?"

"Of course Sameer sahib, you can make as many requests as you like." Rawat seemed to be enjoying himself.

"Can you please not question her at her house? Her husband is—"

"Oh Sameer sahib's lady friend is married also." Singh chuckled.

"Wah, sir ji!" Rawat laughed. "*Bade rangeen tabiyat nikle aap.* Having a good time with a married lady friend!"

"None of your business!" Sameer burst out in anger, standing up.

The remainder of the smile on Rawat's face evaporated as he ground his jaw and locked eyes with Sameer.

"Rawat sahib, why don't we call her here? Sameer *sahib ka mood bhi achha ho jaayega,*" Singh said.

Sameer sat back down, his fists clenched. He hated the thought of Ritu in the police station. But then, it was better than her interrogation at home.

Rawat's eyes burrowed into Sameer, gauging the tumult in his mind. "*Theek hai* Singh. Let's call her here. Let's also meet Sameer sahib's lady friend," He said, "Malviya Nagar, she should get here in about twenty minutes -"

"At this time, she must be at work in CP. It'll take longer." Sameer bit his tongue as soon as he said it.

Rawat's eyes glinted, "Achha, she works in CP too. Where in CP, Sameer sahib?"

Sameer didn't respond. *What have I done?*

"Address, sir ji."

He gave away the Stonewell address.

"Ah, she works in your office," he said, exchanging a look with Singh, "*Phir toh,* we should go and meet her there."

"Please, I beg you. Let's call her here." Sameer folded his hands.

A cruel smile played on Rawat's lips as he stubbed his cigarette in the spherical steel ashtray on his table. "We'll save her the commute."

Rawat and Singh looked around the reception area of the office. Rawat's eyes roamed everywhere. On the wall right to the reception desk were two large paintings of street scenes of London and Delhi. They were done by a British and an Indian artist respectively, symbolizing the link between Stonewell's origins and India operations. The Victorian buildings, mini cabs and glitzy display windows of James Street made a striking contrast with the choking liveliness of Chandni Chowk – cycle rickshaws, ramshackle buildings, colourful signboards and Jama Masjid in the background. Two clocks below the paintings showed the time in London and Delhi. There was a marble sculpture of a horse head in the sitting area where a few black leather sofas had been put up for visitors.

Mitali was at the reception and was surprised to see Sameer with the policemen. After exchanging a brief greeting with her, Sameer said, "I need a favour. These guys," he nodded towards Rawat and Singh, "need to ask a few questions to close a case file. Routine stuff. They want to start with Ritu. Can you send her to the Himalaya?"

Himalaya was the conference room adjacent to the reception. Named so because it was always too cold.

Not everyone in the office will have to see these jokers.

"Ritu?" Mitali asked.

"Yes," he said, walking towards Rawat. "I will take them to Himalaya."

Rawat stood looking at the London painting. "London. *Aap to aate jaate honge,* Sameer sahib. *Hamne to bas filmon mein hi dekha hai.*"

"Sameer…," Mitali called after him as they moved towards Himalaya, "I forgot. Himalaya is occupied. Srini is meeting with a client team."

"What other conference room—"

Rawat interjected, "Madam ji, we don't need a big conference room. Why don't you take us to where she's sitting?"

No.

Rawat sensed Sameer's unease and glanced at Singh to share his amusement.

"It won't be appropriate to talk to her in front of everyone. We'll find a conference room—" Sameer said.

"Please." Rawat raised his hand to cut him off, stone-faced. "I don't think *you* are best qualified to tell us what's appropriate and what's not."

That shut him up.

"*Chaliye* madam," Rawat said, smiling at Mitali. She looked at Sameer, for a sign, but he looked down, surrendering. She started walking towards the office entrance with Rawat and Singh behind her. Sameer followed.

"Very nice office, madam," Rawat said, as he walked through the hallway.

Sameer was conscious of the questioning eyes behind the cubicles.

"Ritu," Mitali called to her softly, as they reached her cubicle. Ritu's head was tilted slightly to the right, her three middle fingers on her forehead, as she peered at her computer screen.

She heard Mitali the second time and lifted her head, her eyes still glazed. She saw the policemen and seemed confused.

Mitali nodded at Sameer and left.

There was only one visitor chair in her cubicle. Since none of them showed any inclination to sit, she stood up. She looked so vulnerable standing there. He had an urge to hold her and protect her from those men.

"Are you Mrs Ritu Mathur?" Singh began.

"Yes." Her voice was tentative, as if she wasn't quite sure of her name.

"*Toh aap hain* Ritu madam." Rawat ran an appreciative eye over her body. "Very nice to meet you."

"We need to ask you a few questions," Rawat said.

"Sure. Perhaps we can sit." Ritu pointed towards Ketan's room; he was out of the country.

"*Nahin,* madam. It'll take five minutes," Rawat had probably grasped how much more damaging it could be to question her there than behind the door of a closed room.

"Can you tell us if Mr Sameer was with you on August 28?"

"Yes."

"A little louder, madam. I didn't hear it." Singh had his file open, his pen poised.

"Yes," she said again, her ears reddening.

It was like the entire office had come to a standstill. Even Kumar's keyboard was silent.

"From what time to what time?" Rawat asked, and then added, "Approximately?" to ensure she answered the question.

"From noon to around six in the evening." He could feel the burning in her eyes.

He hated himself for causing her this humiliation.

"Was there anyone else at the house at that time?" Singh asked.

"No." Her voice had dipped again.

"Louder, madam," Singh said, pretending to be recording the conversation in the file.

"No," she said again, louder this time.

"*Likh liya* Singh? Mr Sameer Chadha was at Mrs Ritu Mathur's house on August twenty eighth from noon to around six in the evening – the day his wife died. And they were alone in the house," he said loudly, trying to reach as many people as he could.

He smiled triumphantly at Sameer. "*Bas, Sameer sahib. Ho gaya.*"

As they left, Ritu coiled back into her chair, staring at her computer screen. Sameer walked both of them back to the elevators, conscious of the scandalized looks he received on the way.

As Singh held the elevator for him, Rawat smiled at Sameer. "Sameer sahib," he said, "*Now* you know my kind."

Tania Chadha Ko
Gussa Kyon Aata Hai.

Tania awoke to the news of Dad being taken away to the police station. Ammaji, who looked weird wearing Tania's old shirt with '# Swagg' printed on the front, couldn't refrain from voicing her unsought opinions. "Someone should have gone with him," she said, "Delhi police can turn an atheist into a priest." She didn't believe Daadu's explanation of a routine enquiry. "He doesn't get Delhi." She shook her head.

Tania didn't know whether to believe her. Ammaji's list of prejudices was long. All garbage collectors were thieves, Bengalis made good doctors, drivers had loose morals.

At breakfast, Daadi struggled with the jam bottle. Tania took it from her and tapped it lightly on the corner of the table and the seal broke. *Dad's trick.* She felt bad for not having spoken with him since her mother's death. He was hurting too. When he came back, she would hug him and cry her heart out.

Naanu sat alone on Pari's bed. He seemed to have aged in the last few days. When he arrived from Chandigarh, the night of her mother's death, he had cried like a baby. Tania went and sat down next to him, holding his hand. He smiled and patted her hand.

"Naanu, tell me a story about Mom."

He stroked her head. "What do you want to hear?"

"Anything."

He told her stories she had heard many times before. Her Mom's pretend friend, her obsession with rabbits and Hema Malini, when she wanted a moustache like her Dad. They wrapped themselves in the warm blanket of her memories; the person they had loved the most. His daughter, her mother.

They sat together in silence after he had run out of stories.

"Tania," he said, breaking the stillness, "Did your Mom and Dad…" he hesitated before completing his question, "have fights lately?"

She was startled by his question. "Why would you think that?"

"I don't understand why the police are after your father."

She lifted her head to look at him. A broken old man, tormented by his daughter's death. "No, Naanu. Mom and Dad were very happy together. I never saw them fight for as long as I can remember. Mom died peacefully, knowing all of us loved her."

She was glad she didn't tell her Mom of the SMS. It was good she went happy, not knowing.

It was past noon when they saw Dad step out of a taxi and climb the stairs. Pari ran to hug him as he came through the door of the apartment. He looked harangued though; sweat spots on his shirt, necktie askew, hair dishevelled.

"What happened?" Daadu asked.

"Routine enquiry. It's over." He ran his fingers through his hair, tousling them even more.

"The policeman at the station told us they took you to your office." Daadu looked up at him. Naanu and Daadu had gone to the police station to enquire about him when he didn't return in the morning.

Naanu shuffled to the living room and sat on the sofa next to Daadu. Pari sat in Daadi's lap.

"Nothing. They wanted to confirm I was there at the time of Kavita's death," Dad said, removing his jacket and loosening the neck tie.

But he wasn't.

"Absurd! Why would they want to enquire that? Kavita died of natural causes," Daadu said.

"Another way to make money." He shook his head with a touch of annoyance. "Someone gave them an opportunity to poke their noses into our tragedy." He glanced at Tania standing near the book case and then looked away.

There had been accusation in his eyes. She asked, "What did I do?"

"Nothing," he said, looking at the wall.

"Tell me."

"You said things you shouldn't have. At the hospital." He still looked at the wall, at that stupid painting of the frowning tribal woman she had never liked. It was like he was having a conversation with her instead of Tania.

She remembered then. She hadn't known someone would pick up her words and use them against him. "I didn't know—"

"It wasn't responsible."

That stung her. *She* was irresponsible? *She* was the one who had rushed her mother to the hospital in the pouring rain. *She* was the one who was forced to make life and death decisions. If there was someone irresponsible, it was *him*. He was the one who had switched his phone off, when his wife lay dying.

"And *you* are responsible?" She said, her voice trembling with fury. Her eyes flashed and colour rose in her cheeks. Turning to her grandfather, she said, "Daadu, why don't you ask him where he was when Mom died."

"Shut up, Tania! You have caused enough trouble with your histrionics," Dad turned to her.

"Why don't you explain where you were at the time? I called you a hundred times, but you didn't pick up." Tears streaming down her face, she stomped out of the room, shouting amidst the stunned silence of the room. "Whatever you may be thinking Dad, no one, *no one* will take the place of my mom. Ever."

They were in the school auditorium, a bunch of them gathered around the stage. An Improv session of the drama club.

"Son, it's good to see you studying hard," said Saumya patting Tanuj on his head as he sat looking down at the table in front, hands on his cheeks. "What do you want to be when you grow up?"

"An auto-rickshaw driver."

Saumya managed to keep a straight face. "What a noble profession to aspire to. Your Dad would have been so proud."

Tanuj got up from the chair, and bowed before the imaginary picture of his father on the wall. *"Pitaji, mujhe aashirwaad dijiye. Aaj maine aapka sapna poora kar diya."*

Miss Ray clapped twice. Tania's turn.

It was her responsibility to change the scene. She went and tapped on Tanuj's shoulder, a signal for him to get off the stage. Saumya sat in the chair Tanuj had vacated. The stage was bare except for a couple of chairs and tables. They were all the props they could use. Tania's eyes caught the feather earrings Saumya wore.

"Who's your stylist?" Tania asked.

"Manish Malhotra," Saumya replied, without batting an eyelid, and made motions to put make-up on her face, peering at the non-existent mirror in front of her.

Tania grabbed the other chair in the room, and sat parallel to her, also putting on some imaginary make-up. "I never work with anyone but Sabyasachi. People say I look most beautiful in a sari. What do you think?"

"I think you're ugly." Saumya crinkled her nose.

"Then how come Karan Johar signed me up for twenty crores?"

"Because I turned him down for lack of dates."

She heard the sharp two claps again. Dhruv came on the stage and tapped on Saumya's shoulder. He stood behind Tania holding her chair, looking at their imaginary reflection in the fictional mirror. "Even after twenty-five years of marriage, you still look every bit as beautiful as when I first met you."

"But not you. You are fat, bald and… gassy."

Dhruv suppressed a smile, as others watching them laughed. "But I still love you."

"I don't. I want a divorce."

"What about the kids?"

Miss Ray clapped thrice signalling Saumya and Tanuj to get back to the stage.

"What about them? They are happily settled. One an actress, the other an auto-rickshaw driver."

Saumya said, "Mom, don't leave us. Please."

Dhruv signalled them to come closer, and held all of them in a group hug. "We are one happy, gassy family."

Miss Ray clapped four times. End of the scene.

"Good job, guys." Miss Ray high-fived them one by one. She grinned at Tania. "Gassy… really?"

Tania packed her things and walked towards the parking lot for the school bus. It was her first week back at school. Everyone seemed to feel sorry for her. She wondered if her mother's death had scared them, made them realize it could happen to them too.

Her thoughts drifted to Naanu who left after her little scene with Dad. She pleaded with him to stay, but he said he needed to get away. She hadn't intended to create a scene in front of the entire family. She didn't know what came over her. One minute she was worried about her Dad and the next she lashed out at him.

"Tania!" Dhruv called out. He sprinted to catch up with her, a mop of curls across his forehead. She stopped. "Very sorry about your mom," he said, breathing hard, when he caught up with her.

Tania still hadn't figured the response to this standard line. She stayed silent. They walked together side by side. The school was quiet; drama club had been an after-school activity.

"I wanted to say we're friends... and... I'm there for you. If you want to talk or something."

She looked at him and knew he meant it. She was touched by his gesture.

Looking out of the window, as the school bus weaved its way home through the traffic – honking cars, dusty roads, and bustling markets – she thought about him. *The* Dhruv considered her a friend. She allowed herself a tiny smile.

Chhoti Si Baat

Revathi, the self-appointed leader of the group, mouthed, "One, two, three, four." Manik started on the bass guitar. The audience recognized the prelude to the *India waale*. Diminutive Jasleen, probably the most accomplished player of the group, was next, on the drums, picking up the beat. Revathi and Aayush joined in on keyboard and guitar at the same time. It was amazing to see them responding to each other. Theoretically, autism made it difficult to have group interactions. But melody trumped it. The music they played was seamless.

Aayush's voice filled the hall, seconds later, as the instruments slowed to make space for him, the lead singer of the group. As always, his singing gave Ritu goose bumps. His eyes weren't on the audience, but on the lyrics sheet in front of him, as he swayed on his feet from side to side. Nonetheless, the chemistry between the rock group and the audience – a motley group of parents and their friends – was instantaneous.

Halfway through the song, the rhythmic clapping began. She looked at Sameer joining in, caught in the magic of the moment. The audience burst into a big applause when the song ended. Revathi signalled to the others and they all took a bow.

And then, they were on to the next song.

When the performance ended, amidst the congratulations and smiles, Revathi's parents took charge of the rock band. They wanted to treat them all to dinner.

"McDonald's," said Revathi, her hands flapping, trying hard to keep herself calm, amidst all the excitement.

Sameer and Ritu slipped to Café Coffee Day adjacent to McDonald's where the band was celebrating. The aroma of roasted coffee beans was warm, comforting. When he called in the morning to say he wanted to meet, she had asked him home. But she sensed his reluctance; he was burning in the same hell of guilt as her. Ritu then suggested he join her for the concert at Aayush's school in the evening.

"I'm so sorry for yesterday... I wish it hadn't happened," he said, as he put her macchiato and his latté on the table and sat down across her.

So did she. But it had. She squeezed his hand lightly over the table. The turquoise stone of her ring sparkled in the light of the lamp.

"What are you going to do?" he asked her, sipping from his cup.

She didn't know.

After Sameer left with the policemen, she had sent a leave application to Ketan, picked up her things and walked out of the office. She had no clue how she was ever going to get back and look those people in the eyes again. Throughout their relationship, she had been audacious. She had thought she wouldn't care if people found out. But now, she felt exposed, vulnerable.

She told him she had taken leave for a week.

Sameer replied, "I have to go tomorrow. Public issue coming up. Can't even take leave."

"Sameer, there's something I have to tell you."

"Yeah?"

She looked into his eyes. "I'm pregnant."

Aaj ki Taaza Khabar

"What?" The coffee cup in Sameer's hand froze on its way to his lips.

"You heard me." Her eyes bored into his. That unflinching, unblinking gaze that made him uneasy.

"I thought you were on the pill."

"I got off during the safe period."

Not safe enough. "What're you going to do now?"

"I don't know."

He put the cup down and wiped the spill with the paper napkin. He realized he had made a faux pas on the *you;* he wanted to say something to make it better, but couldn't think of anything. Eventually, he blurted, "We'll find a way. I have a friend in Holy Child – he could refer us to a good gynecologist for abortion—"

"I didn't say I wanted to abort."

What? "What do you want to do?"

"I don't know."

What did she know then?

That conversation hadn't gone too well, Sameer thought, as he drove to the office. He should have been more supportive. But he had felt ambushed; she had just sprung the news on him.

The car moved sluggishly in the morning traffic on Ashoka Road. *Hundreds of little steel cocoons ferrying their passengers to destinations they hated.* Sameer wanted to know more. How far along was she, when did she find out and how long did she take to tell him? But she had shut him out of the conversation with her cryptic 'I don't knows'.

The light on Barakhamba Road turned red as Sameer was about to cross and he braked sharply, inviting horns from the cars behind him. *Still, I should have been gentler.* It must be a major emotional upheaval for her.

Sameer sat still in his car after parking. Not quite ready to face the office.

He had come in early; he wanted to get in unnoticed. Finally, he got out and walked to his office. After entering the reception area, he walked briskly to his room, looking straight ahead, ignoring the usual early birds, and closed the door behind him. The public issue was a couple of weeks away and there was a lot to do. Losing himself in work was the only way to keep sane. To escape the all-consuming quicksand of remorse.

His office was even messier than usual. His in-tray overflowed – correspondence from merchant bankers and underwriters on the public issue, budget projections for the next year, auditors' schedule. Neena had stacked all financial reports on the table, a mini hill of paper. Two folders with urgent tabs sat on his chair.

As the day progressed, interactions with others became necessary. He called Neena, who looked as disoriented as ever, mismatched clothes, hair frayed. She left immediately after they finished, as if she couldn't bear to be in the same room as him.

At eleven, he met with his full team – Kartik, Neha, Arjun and Neena. Kartik wore his usual smirk and tried to be smart on a couple of occasions. Off colour jokes about Sameer's first-hand knowledge of inner workings of Ketan's office – a reference to Ritu.

The phone rang as he finished his lunch of a chicken salad sandwich delivered to his room. Single ring; an outside call.

"Mr. Sameer Chadha?"

"Yes?"

"This is Nikhil Roy from *Financial News*. I'm doing a feature on Stonewell's public issue. Can I speak with you for a few minutes?"

Nikhil Roy. Wow. One of the best known financial journalists in Delhi. Sameer sat upright. "Mr Roy, perhaps it would be best if you spoke with Mr Ketan Pandit, our CFO. He's out of the country, but will be back later this week."

"I know Mr Pandit is out of the country. He suggested I talk to you. I have a few basic questions about your last quarter's financial statements."

That didn't sound good.

Pause.

"This shouldn't take more than ten minutes," Roy persisted.

I am going to get screwed.

Roy began, "Interestingly, Stonewell reports a twenty-seven percent increase in sales and the margins are better too while the industry trends for most pharmaceutical companies producing basic drugs are downwards—"

The pen in his hand doodled a jagged line on the writing pad in front of him. "Mr Roy, I really don't know the market too well. Perhaps, you would want to talk to someone in marketing."

"But a twenty-seven percent increase in sales, when the industry average is a decline of twelve percent?"

"I know… I mean I don't know. I'm not the best person to talk to about this."

"Do you think you could send me the details of the sales statements so that I can look up the top sellers? It would help my feature."

He stopped drawing. "They are on the company website along with the published results."

"Thanks for your time, Mr Chadha."

Whew. His palms were sweaty.He exhaled deeply and focused his attention on the tasks related to the public issue.

Around five in the evening, his phone rang again, after he had concluded a long discussion with SBI Capital Markets. It was Roy again.

"Mr Chadha, thanks for referring me to your website. Very useful. I have a couple of follow up questions. I hope you don't mind."

Oh, I do mind. But I don't have a choice. You don't say no to Nikhil Roy.

"In the top sellers, I see two brands – Insusave and Wavetor – which I believe are anti-diabetic and cardiovascular drugs. I thought Stonewell hadn't ventured into those categories. Can you please clarify?"

Holy crap.

He squeezed his eyes shut. "Are you there, Mr Chadha?"

"Aah…yes."

"I thought I had lost you there. So are these drugs in Stonewell's repertoire now?"

"These details come from sales people. I can connect you to them, if you want." He rubbed his forehead with his fingers.

"That may not be necessary," Roy said. "I've done my research. These are Bio-chem products, which is an allied company. Wasn't too hard. All it required was a visit to the chemist around the corner."

Oh god!

"I have one more question for you. Did Stonewell acquire a majority stake in Bio-Chem before March? My information is it was done in May – and probably you are best placed to answer this question – not the sales people."

Sameer sat frozen.

"Mr Chadha?"

"You're… right."

"*I am?* I see. Bio-chem sales have been included in Stonewell financial statements for March even though Stonewell's shareholding in the company at that point was less than fifty percent…"

He continued, after a pause, not getting any rebuttal, "…which is contrary to Companies Law, tax laws and in direct violation of SEBI guidelines… unless of course I am unaware of any sweeping changes made in laws you'd like to enlighten me with."

Sameer's temples throbbed as he tried the escalate-and-delay tactic once more. "Mr Roy, I am afraid these are issues on which I have no authority to speak. I suggest you talk to the CFO or Director Finance—"

"I don't think there's a need," Roy responded. "And besides, you would perhaps remember, you signed those financial statements."

The Chance card in Monopoly. Go directly to Jail. Do not pass Go.
"But…"

"I can't believe a company like Stonewell stooped to an action so clumsy, so crude. What were you thinking?"

"Please listen. I'll talk to the Board – we'll withdraw these statements…" He stood up.

"Don't you think it's a bit late for that? Whatever you do, Mr Chadha, please make sure you buy a copy of *Financial News* tomorrow morning. It's going to be sensational."

Darr

Ritu was in deep sleep when she felt his hand cupping her breast. Half asleep, she turned to him. Then his hand was up her negligee, between her legs, exploring roughly. She opened her eyes, startled. *Sunil.*

There hadn't been physical intimacy between them the last few months. Without saying anything, he had stopped sleeping in their bedroom and crashed either with Aayush in his room, or on the sofa in the living room, often with the TV blaring all night.

What is he doing in the bedroom today? She removed his hand and turned to the other side, pretending to sleep. *Here is your signal, bozo. Go away.*

After a minute, his hand was again up her legs, from behind, mauling her buttocks.

"Stop it," she said curtly.

He forced her to turn to his side again. His breath reeked of whisky. In the dim light of the night bulb, she could see the drunken obstinacy on his face.

"Why?"

"Go fuck one of your sluts. Leave me alone."

That was a bad idea.

He was on top of her, forcing her legs apart, his hands roughing up her breasts as he tried to kiss her on the lips. He disgusted her. She pushed him off with all her strength and climbed out of the bed.

"What's wrong with you? Get the fuck out of here," she shouted.

Her anger ignited his. "What's wrong with *me*? What's wrong with *you*? Why can't I have sex with my wife?" He got out of the bed and glared at her.

"Please, Sunil. I've had a bad day." She held out her hands.

He pinned her against the wall, his body crushing hers. He tried to pin her face down to kiss her on the lips, as she kept it moving side to side. She kneed him hard between his legs. He yelped in surprise and pain and let go of her. She leapt towards the door, but he reached in time to wedge his foot before she could close it behind her. In the living room, he grabbed her by her hair. "Bitch, you hurt me."

"Please, Sunil. I'm sorry." She tried to loosen his grip on her hair.

He shoved her hard towards the dining table, knocking her against the chairs. One of the chair legs broke and its edge caught her upper arm; her head hit the edge of the table and throbbed with pain.

"Please, Sunil. I'm sorry. Please don't hurt me," she pleaded with him in panic as he advanced towards her.

She spotted Aayush standing at the door of his room, confused. The noise must have woken him up.

"Aayush, call the police… you know how… dial 100," she said hysterically.

Sunil shouted, "Aayush, go back to your room."

"Aayush, please…he will kill me…"

"In your room! Now!" Sunil shouted.

For a moment, Aayush seemed to hesitate. Then he ran inside his room, his arms flapping, and bolted the door.

"You want police in this house!" He slapped her hard on the cheek. "You'll learn to listen to me!"

His lips were on hers. She lay there like a log of wood, defeated; waiting for it to be over. Her lack of response enraged him further. He bit her lips. She moaned in pain. "Useless bitch! Can't even please a man."

"You're no man." She seethed, despite herself.

"I'll kill you!" He strangled her incensed.

"Sttooppp…," she whispered as his grip around her neck grew tighter and she flailed her arms uselessly.

She heard the knocking on the door first. His grip on her neck slackened when it got louder. Taking advantage of his confusion, she pushed him off her and ran limping towards the door, her body hurting from the effort. There were two uniformed policemen at the door. The shorter one at the front said, "We had a call from here—"

She didn't have to say anything. Her torn clothes, her bloodied arm, his drunken state spoke it all. She broke down with relief.

Aayush opened the door of his room. She ran towards him and hugged him. "You called the police. You listened to Mama."

"Aayush listen both Daddy and Mama. Daddy say go into room. Aayush go into room. Mama says call police. Aayush call police."

Maa, Where Are You?

*S*he is nine. They are in the park – her mother, sister and her. Tania sits on the swing wearing her favourite dress of tiny white daisies and asks her mother to push, to make her soar in the sky. The swing goes higher and higher. She sees the sky, deep blue, with whipped cream clouds. And then sees the earth as the swing comes back. Sky and earth. Blue and brown. Blue. Brown. Blue. Brown.

Her sister, a cranky two-year-old, who everyone surprisingly finds cute, wants to go home. Her mother asks her if she wants to leave too. She doesn't; she is giddy with the flying. Her sister starts crying. Since she arrived in their life, she has snatched her mom from her. It is always her sister. She needs milk now. She wants to play now. She needs to sleep now. It's always her.

Tania doesn't want to go home. And she doesn't want her mom to go either.

But there is her mom, giving in to her sister's tantrum again. Her mom tells her she'll be back. Other moms are all there. Only her mom has to go back. Parul's maid is pushing Tania on the swing now. Off she goes, higher and higher. But it is not fun any longer. She looks at her mom and sister leave the turnstile exit of the park. Her posture has shifted, she is watching where they are, not where she is. And suddenly as the swing goes up, she doesn't see the sky. Instead, she sees the earth hurtling towards her. She is on the ground and everybody is crowded *around her. She's crying. As much from the pain, as from the shame of having fallen down in front of everyone. Her dress is muddy and her forehead sticky. There is blood.*

She is inconsolable. And then she smells her. Even before she hears her voice or sees her. Then she knows she is safe. Her sister is nowhere to be seen as her mother picks her up and runs out of the park. She is in the car, her head in her mother's lap, her mother's dupatta pressed against her forehead.

She is in the hospital and it smells of Dettol. The doctor too. He says she needs stitches. She is sure they are going to hurt, whatever they are. She cries and shakes her head; she doesn't want them.

It turns out they are even more painful than she had thought. She holds her mother's arm tight, very tight, as the dettol doctor puts the needle in her skin. Four times. Her nails dig into her mother's arm a little harder each time. She would see the bruise on her mom's arm later and be surprised it was her work.

She wakes up at home to find her mom sitting right next to her. Her mom smiles and touches her cheek. She doesn't see her sister anywhere and is pleased to have mom all to herself. She has a fever; she hears something about an infection. She sleeps a lot. But when she awakes, she finds her mom at her bedside. Three days and three nights. She goes back to sleep, feeling secure, knowing her mother is watching over her.

Tania's fingers traced the now faint scar on her forehead. *How I miss you, Mom.*

The mornings were the hardest. After a night of turning off the conscious, waking up to remember she was gone. The hope of each new dawn crushed by that brutal reality. Or when she came home in the school bus, and thought of narrating her day to Mom.

It ought to be a gradual process – the passing of a person. She should be allowed a phone call to Mom once a day. Then once a week, later once a month, before her mother was allowed to disappear permanently. She needed to get used to her absence. The abruptness of her departure was too hard to bear.

She was on the balcony, sitting in her mother's favourite chair and ran her fingers over the palm frond, the taller one, her mother named Tania. She watched a drop of water roll off the ribbed surface of the palm and closed her eyes. That was how she remembered her best, reclining in this chair, her feet on the table, a book in hand.

She looked at the shorter palm on the far side and thought of Pari. She had been awfully quiet since Mom's death. The day before, she had refused to go to Shreya's birthday party, despite Tania's persuasions.

She got up and walked over to Pari's room. She was asleep. She looked cute with her face resting on her two hands held together and her knees pulled to her stomach. Tania caressed her cheek and turned around to leave. Realizing suddenly that Pari had felt hot, she rebounded and felt her forehead. It was burning; Pari had a fever.

"Pari!" she touched her arm.

No response.

She called Ammaji for a thermometer.

"Pari!" She shook her roughly.

"W-h-a-t?"

The temperature was over hundred and four.

She found Crocin, poured it in the measuring spoon and put it to Pari's lips. "Drink it."

Giving her medicine had never been easy. Pari shook her head and tried to slip back to sleep.

"You have to!"

In her half-asleep state, Pari recognized authority and drank it. She made a sour face and went back to sleep.

What else?

She thought of wet presses her Mom used to apply when either Pari or Tania had high fever. She asked Ammaji for water and a couple of hand towels and soon both of them were placing the water soaked pieces of cloth on the exposed parts of Pari's body, with Pari fighting back with all the strength she could muster.

Half an hour. She checked the temperature again. It hadn't decreased.

A wave of panic shot through her. Ammaji was wringing her hands, when, with a foreboding sense of déjà vu, she called Dad.

One ring. Two. Three. Four. Five. *This can't be happening again. Please pick up the phone, Dad.*

"Hello."

When she told him, he was all alert, all action. "I'm starting now. We've got to take her to Sanjeevani. Ask Dayal to come up and help you carry her down. I'll call them to see if they have a pediatrician available."

He was in charge. Everything would be alright.

At the nursing home, they were expecting Pari's arrival. The pediatrician, Dr Mehra, was in attendance. He was a tall man with big hands. In the narrow examination room, with the single white painted steel cot and barely any standing room, he supervised, as the nurse checked Pari's temperature and then took her blood sample.

Then her Dad arrived and there was activity. Questions, answers, consultations.

"We'll need to carry out tests to determine if it's a viral or a bacterial infection. It could be dengue that hasn't been attended to for a few days and has gotten worse."

Dengue, the killer. Over two hundred killed in Delhi.

Pari was shifted to another small, bare room, with no windows. The white sheets on the bed were cool in contrast to Pari's burning skin.

Her Dad would stay with Pari for the night. Tania wanted to stay too, but he overruled her; someone had to be home. However, he wanted her to take care of Pari, while he went to collect his things.

Pari lay on the bed, an antibiotic drip attached to her arm, restless. Tania watched her, holding her free hand, caressing her forehead.

That night, Tania was restless. In her dreams, images of Mom and Pari juxtaposed. She woke up and lay waiting for dawn. As soon as it was light, she rushed to the hospital. Her Dad sat on a chair beside Pari; his eyes reflecting the fear in hers. The news wasn't good. The fever hadn't broken and her platelet count was down. *It was dengue.*

She heard of steroids and stronger anti-pyretic medication. Dr Mehra wasn't as calm as the day before; the blood test results had been worse than expected. By evening, even though the steroids seemed to be working and the platelets count was better, the fever was still high. Her Dad was exploring the option of shifting her to another hospital.

In the night, she shook her head when Dad asked her to leave. He acquiesced, told her to take the couch. They watched over Pari together, taking turns resting, neither of them able to sleep. The minute hand of the wall clock above the couch made a grating sound each time it moved.

Pari flitted in and out of consciousness. The fever fluctuated. Dr Mehra made a midnight appearance, the stethoscope hanging from his neck like a talisman. He looked up her medication chart and made adjustments.

In the early hours of the morning, Pari mumbled in her sleep. Tania couldn't decipher the words, but she heard Pari say Mom. Tears streamed down her face as she hugged Pari. *Come back, Pari. To the land of the living. I need you.*

Fire

Propped against the pillows, Ritu took a gulp of the milk-and-turmeric concoction her mother had brought her. As she stretched for a paper tissue to wipe the rim of the chipped Nescafe mug, pain shot through her shoulder and she grimaced.

"Still hurts?" Her mother sat down beside her.

She shook her head. "Much better."

"I can't believe you never told us."

Her parents had been content in the illusion of her blissful marriage; she hadn't seen the point of disrupting their fantasy.

After the policemen took her to the hospital that night, she had called her father. He was so agitated that she started to worry for him. She called him a second time, as a nurse dressed the laceration on her arm. "Everything's fine. The doctors say I'll be out in the morning."

Then she had called Sameer, who stayed with Aayush and her till she was discharged the next morning.

Sunil was out on bail. Even though the restraining orders were in place, she feared going back to their apartment. It felt safer in her parents' place with the warm blanket of security of neighbours they had known for decades.

Ritu hugged Aayush as he wriggled out of her embrace. He was almost as tall as she. "Mama's so proud of Aayush."

"Aayush so proud of Mama too." He parroted after her.

Aayush had been accepted to London's Royal Academy of Music for a diploma in music performance. The confirmation had come in that morning. They had applied to a number of music schools that ran special courses for autistic kids. Rejection after rejection; she had given up hope. And then she heard from one of the best.

Aayush would receive lessons from an experienced teacher through video conferencing for a year. This could prepare him for an undergraduate degree in music from the same school, if they chose to pursue it.

The kettle let out a soft whistle. She took it off the stove and poured out a cup of tea for herself.

Her one-week-turned-two month long absence from the office was ending soon and she hated the thought of going back to work, to face the scorn of her colleagues.

Que sera sera. No point in brooding about it. At least today.

She got up and knocked on the door of her parents' bedroom; the door was bolted from the inside.

"What?" Aayush shouted.

"Open the door. Mama needs to talk."

"No hugging?"

"No hugging."

He opened the door a crack, saw her at a safe distance and stepped out. She ran and hugged him again.

"Mama!" he protested.

She leaned her head back and laughed.

The lawyers had reached a settlement. It had three main clauses. First, Ritu and Sunil would file for a divorce with mutual consent.

Second, Ritu would withdraw the police case against Sunil. In return, Sunil would move out of the house. Third, Ritu would have Aayush's custody but Sunil could see him on weekends. Ritu's safety would be ensured by the restraining orders on Sunil continuing to be in place. The settlement papers were to be signed that day and they had agreed to meet at her lawyer's office at noon.

Aayush had asked her about Sunil a few times; the violence of that night forgotten in his mind. She tried preparing him for the eventuality of separating from Sunil for good. He nodded his head vigorously when she asked if he understood. But she wasn't sure if he really did.

The sound of guitar music floated into the room; Aayush was practicing. It surprised her how much more at home he was here than her, the house *she* had grown up in. She depended on him to find things – towel, soap, sugar. Her parents and Aayush had perfected a harmony, their roles clear. Aayush set the table, her mother served. Her father bought the groceries, Aayush carried the bags.

Growing up, Ritu hated everything about the house. The white paint peeling off the walls, the doors you struggled to shut, the bathroom faucet that needed to be twisted four times, back and forth, for the dripping to stop, the lack of space.

They had moved into the tiny two-room government apartment in Sarojini Nagar when her father got himself transferred from Etawah to Delhi. She had been a stick-thin ten-year-old. She had pleasant memories of Etawah. Of climbing guava trees, digging out fresh turnips from the kitchen garden, sleeping on the terrace in summer and being woken by rain.

Her father, Shri Kedar Nath Srivastava, Assistant Director, Ministry of Health and Family Welfare, didn't vacate the flat even after retirement – he was defending a suit for eviction filed by the government. Everything was old and musty; a wet odor of decay hung in the air. The furniture was battered, the paintings on the wall discoloured, the refrigerator waged a losing battle to keep things cold. She had fought with her mother to replace some of the things. The sofa in the living room, for instance, where cushions had been placed strategically to hide where the cloth had given way to use of more than twenty years, the dishes which bore marks of food eaten years ago. But her mother had always won. *Her winning argument – there was no need.*

She had always been like this, her mother. The goddess of frugality. Nothing ever got wasted in their home. The old newspapers became covers for her text books and sold for cash, along with used shampoo bottles. Used paint boxes became buckets in the bathroom, milk tins turned into flower pots with money plants that never brought in the dough they were supposed to. Slithers of Lifebuoy soap continued to be used till they disappeared altogether, toothpaste tubes were split open with scissors to ensure every last bit was used.

She opened the doors of the creaky steel cupboard to look for clothes to wear and sighted a cockroach, its antennas moving up and down. With a rolled up newspaper, she flicked it out. *I want to go home.* She looked through the few clothes she had bought and selected a sequined black top that showed her curves and powder-blue jeans to go with it. *Let the moron see what he was losing.*

As they entered the lawyer's office in Bhikaji Cama Place, a pretty girl at the reception directed them to the meeting room. Sunil and his lawyer were there already. Ritu's lawyer, a middle-aged portly man, Malhotra, began to explain the terms of the final settlement.

She looked at Sunil; a man sinking deeper and deeper in the morass of his own failings. *Aren't circumstances the villain in most lives gone wrong?* She remembered the time when he had been full of hope. She remembered the animated discussions they had in the college, their first few years in Indonesia when his dreams started turning to reality. She mourned the demise of that man. This man, shirt spilling out of his trousers where his paunch began, with a stubble of many days and red rimmed alcoholic eyes, she had never loved.

The room was starting to smell of stale breaths. Malhotra continued reading out the terms in a dull monotone. They didn't own any properties that needed to be divided. They had separate bank accounts that each retained. Either of them had no right on the others' salary. Whatever they had in the house would remain there and belong to her.

It was amazing how the closest relationships had in them to turn the most bitter. Father-son, mother-daughter, brother-brother, sister-sister. And then, the most intimate – and the most acrimonious when it did not work – husband and wife. Two people living under the same roof, sharing the same bed, chafing, bristling, snapping at each other's inconsequential provocations. Fighting, scheming in their petty enmity to inflict wounds on the other. Accumulating such anger and hatred for each other that when it boiled over, it was hideous.

She remembered everything. The women, the shame, the physical abuse. The bile of anger rose in her chest. Sunil signed the settlement papers. It was over. She was free.

There was one thing she needed to do however.

"Can I have a word with Sunil alone?" she asked, as she put the last of the series of signatures on the settlement papers.

Sunil seemed surprised. Malhotra got up and opened the door of the meeting room, and gestured to Sunil's lawyer and her father. They got up and filed out of the room, her father, a bit reluctantly.

Sunil looked at her.

She looked directly into his eyes. "One last thing, Sunil. Thought you should know." She smiled. "I am pregnant. And you… are not the father."

The look on his face – priceless.

Game

They watched a movie together at home. Pari and Sameer. She laughed as Ajay Devgan began to get mad at Arshad Warsi showing him a finger; he got out of control if someone did that. She knew what to expect next and laughed in anticipation. He smiled. In her Hello Kitty pink night suit, her hair braided in two pigtails, she looked cute hugging her knees and giggling uncontrollably.

The scare she gave him. He lived a nightmare in those thirty-six hours. A nightmare within the nightmare his life had become.

The morning after Dr Mehra's midnight visit, she regained consciousness for the first time. He sat in the chair beside her bed, looking at her sleeping. The nursing home was coming alive; morning greetings being exchanged, floors being scrubbed, breakfast trolleys making their rounds. Pari mumbled something and he bent to listen, but couldn't hear what she said.

"Pari, did you say something?"

She sat up, her right hand moving horizontally in the air. "I said why didn't you go to office today?" Her voice was loud and clear.

He held her small body in a tight embrace. "Because I love you too much."

Tania, who lay on the couch sleepless, joined them in the hug.

The last few days that he stayed at home with her, he had seen her turn to Pari of the old – laughing, shouting, playful. He had considered asking his parents to come and help him take care of Pari. But eventually decided against it. She was his responsibility. And he had enjoyed spending time with her.

Tania was away at school. The shared stress of Pari's sickness had brought Tania and him together too. They were finally talking to each other.

He walked over to the balcony to look at the jasmine shrub. A few days ago, he had seen the shiny leaves browning at the ends. He had pruned the dead leaves and watered the plant. He sat down with the organic mulch he had purchased after scouring the internet and applied it to the roots. Then he picked up Kavita's garden scissors and snipped off a few dead leaves before watering it.

Walking back to Pari, he reflected on the horrible situation at work.

Nikhil Roy's article had appeared in the *Financial News* the day after their telephone conversation. It was direct and damning. The resultant tornado was unlike anything he had seen before. The company received a notice for explanation from SEBI the very next day, followed by the arrival of their investigation team. The Company Law Board and the Income Tax Department were on their tail too. Editorials appeared in the newspapers on the culture of corporate fraud. Questions were raised in Parliament over the conduct of foreign companies in India. Some consumer interest groups also joined the chorus.

The company's name was in the mud. In a major embarrassment for the Board, the public issue had to be withdrawn. London was furious. An internal enquiry was initiated to affix responsibilities.

Last week, when Pari felt a little better, he had gone back to work. His isolation at the office was total; he was a pariah no one wanted to interact with. It felt eerie. Caught in his glass cocoon, he sensed a flurry of activity around him and yet he was kept out of it. He soldiered on in the slim hope that truth would prevail. The Finance Director,

Ravi Bansal, who was tasked with the enquiry, interviewed him twice and Sameer recounted the entire story, including his meeting with Ketan to tell him what was going on. It was his word against Ketan's – and the signatures on the financial statements were his. No marks for guessing who would take the hit.

The question was more – what was the hit going to be? Would they let him off easy, make a noise about lack of controls and warn him for the future? Or would they want to make an example of him? Fire him and publicize the action? Repair the damage to the company's name, at his cost.

Bansal was to submit his final report to the Board that day and he had been called to be present at the Board meeting.

He tugged at one of Pari's pigtails. "Pari... I have to go to the office today."

She pressed the pause button on the remote and Ajay Devgan froze on screen. "Do you have to?"

"I'll be back soon." He shrugged his right shoulder where she had laid her head. "We can watch the movie," he said, as he looked at his watch, "for an hour more."

Driving to the office in the afternoon, he felt the tension build in his neck and shoulders. He stopped at the traffic signal at Chirag Delhi flyover. 'Jesus saves' proclaimed the graffiti on the wall. He sure hoped so.

There was a tap on the window. He looked up to see a beaming Imran with his load of books. He wore a shirt with stars and stripes of the American flag with USA written in big bold letters across.

"School *nahin gaya aaj*?" He asked, unrolling the window.

"Half day today. Teacher sick."

Imran flashed him his whitest smile as the traffic light turned green. "Sir, don't worry, be happy."

The Board room was on the eighteenth floor of the office building with a panoramic view of the city. Behind the tall office buildings and commercial bustle of Connaught Place – the heart of Delhi – one could see the green of Lodhi Gardens.

He had been here once before, many years ago, as a rookie. He had sat on the chairs in the back row, behind Mr Prasad, the then CFO, to feed him data. He remembered feeling intimidated in the presence of dour men in dark suits and their aggressive questioning. He felt far more terrified as he sat in the front row now, sweating in his suit, despite the air conditioning.

All the eight Board members were present. Gokhale, the chairperson, whose smiling countenance adorned every annual report, sat at the head of the table. He wasn't smiling right then. The management team was seated on the other side. Srini – the CEO, Ketan, Deshmukh – the HR boss, Nitin, and then him. *In the bloody pecking order.* Ketan gave him his most charming CFO smile when he caught his eye.

Gokhale started the proceedings. "We all know why we're here. The last few weeks have been disastrous for the company and our reputation has taken a major blow. Mr Bansal, who was entrusted with the enquiry, has completed his investigation and will present his findings today."

He nodded to Bansal.

Bansal was a big man and he stretched to his full height. He started in a rather long-winded fashion – the objective of the investigation, the process, the people he met. A whole lot of bull. He tuned out of Bansal's prattle and glanced at Ketan. There was such supreme confidence on the man's face. The polished CFO, looking impeccably groomed in his black pin-striped suit, styled hair, and the clipped french beard. Poised, alert and smart. He sighed. *How are they ever going to take my word against his?*

"...there has been gross negligence all over, starting with the Board. The Board and its secretariat should've exercised due diligence.

The CEO should've carefully scrutinized the statements before sending them to the Board. The CFO of the company should've been more closely involved in the preparation of the financial statements." He paused for a moment, as Sameer waited, nails digging into his palms. "However, the primary responsibility for the negligence lies with Mr Sameer Chadha, Assistant Controller Finance, who signed off on financial statements."

Here we go.

The directors looked in Sameer's direction and their gaze stung him. He realized he had been a fool hoping for leniency from them. They were baying for blood. They needed a scapegoat and he was the perfect choice.

Bansal plodded through his recommendations that included strengthening controls at the Board and top management. More blah.

"My last recommendation is to discharge Mr Chadha from his current responsibilities as his malicious and ill-informed conduct has cost the company its peerless reputation. He has demonstrated he's not equal to the tasks given to him."

It took him a moment to understand. Bansal had been a civil servant before and still spoke the antiquated language – *peerless reputation, malicious and ill-informed conduct, discharge from responsibilities, not equal to the tasks given to him.*

He was to be fired. Let go. End of his career with Stonewell. Finito.

He burned with the unfairness of it all. He looked at Ketan, but Ketan didn't meet his eye. Sameer raised his hand.

"Yes, Mr Chadha?"

"Mr Gokhale. I believe this recommendation is grossly unfair. I've related the entire sequence of events to Mr Bansal, but he hasn't taken it into account in coming to his conclusions—"

"You've had your chance," Bansal interrupted him.

"I had left a note for the Board explaining the situation and informed the CFO when I found the published financial statements included Bio-chem results."

"The Board never got any such note and Mr Pandit denies any knowledge of the issue." Bansal looked at Ketan.

This time, Ketan looked up and held Sameer's gaze. "Mr Chadha is *not* telling the truth. He did *not* tell me that the financial statements included Biochem numbers. I would have withdrawn them if I had known."

The Oscar goes to Mr Ketan Pandit!

Bansal looked at Sameer in vindication. "Besides, your job was to report it *before* you signed off on those statements. You should be glad we are letting you off easy, not pressing charges for personal financial gains in the stock market."

"Which may very well be the case," said Modi, the Board member with the Dawood Ibrahim moustache.

His head throbbed. He leant forward and looked at Ketan, "Someone *did* do this deliberately. But it wasn't me."

Ketan shook his head. "Sameer, what's the point of maligning the entire management like this. Mr Bansal is right – you should be glad we aren't handing you over to police."

Sameer shouted, "I came to your office on the evening of 18 June and…"

Gokhale cut him off. "Mr Chadha, I believe the time for explanations and relating sequence of events is long past. The meeting today is for us to hear about the results of Mr Bansal's investigation into the issue."

He stopped; there was no point. Nothing he said would change their decision.

There was some more inane discussion amongst the Board members and then between the Board members and the management team.

"Mr Srinivas, I trust you'll follow the Board recommendations immediately."

"We will."

So that was it? His eleven-year-old career in Stonewell coming to an abrupt end? Was this how it worked in this cut-throat world of bottom lines? You slaved for years, made each task a life or death affair. Then one day you made a mistake and it was all over.

He had an hour to clear his room. Not much to collect; a few family pictures and some investments papers. Everything else belonged to Stonewell. Sameer closed the door and looked around the room. There were many memories associated with these four walls. His second home. Victories and defeats, accomplishments and disappointments, bonhomie and conflict. None of that mattered any longer. There would be someone else and everything would go on as before. One straw man replaced by another.

He made his way out of the office. He had never thought he would leave like this – escorted by security, a cardboard box in his hand, his eyes downcast.

In front of the elevator, he handed over his access cards to the security.

"Leaving, sir?"

He turned to find Ashok.

"The best of the wishes, sir." Ashok extended his hand.

"Thanks, Ashok ji."

"Sir, what people say, Mr Ashok not believe. You... a good man." Strands of Ashok's flowing beard swayed to a blast of cold air as the elevator door opened.

Sameer's eyes welled up with tears. At least one person believed in him.

Ashok's hand touched his shoulder. "Everything okay sir. Everything fine in future."

As the elevator glided down, the descent of each floor marked by a sliver of sunlight, Sameer looked at the changing numbers, hoping no one would come in and watch him cry.

London Dreams

At the office, Ritu was in for a surprise.

Everyone greeted her like she had returned from a long vacation, hugs and warm smiles all around. No mention of the humiliating episode with the policemen or Sameer. She was overwhelmed by the magnanimity of her colleagues.

Ketan was away on a visit to London and she spent the entire morning taking over from Seema, who had substituted in her absence.

It was in the afternoon, she got to her e-mails. 773 not read. She sighed and started to scan the subjects and the sender. There were few that required action from her. Seema had handled most that were addressed to Ketan. She built up a rhythm as she read and deleted. Read. Delete. Read. Delete. Read. Delete.

She almost missed it. No one paid much attention to mails from HR – mumbo jumbo staff circulars, difficult to comprehend. But the subject line was a job number and she remembered. London office had advertised for a one-year term position and she had applied. She had interviewed on telephone days before the divorce settlement. It had been a particularly bad time and the conversation hadn't gone well.

She paused, leant back on her chair and looked at her computer screen, her hands on the arms of her chair. She didn't even know what she wanted to see.

Whatever. It was what it was.
She leant forward and clicked the mouse.

Dear Ms Mathur,

We are pleased to inform you that you have been selected for the one-year term position of an Executive Assistant in Asia Pacific division based in London. Standard terms and conditions related to term assignments apply and are enclosed in the attachment. Please confirm your acceptance of the assignment within seven days of this mail.

Sincerely yours

Paula Jones, HR Manager,
Asia Pacific Division

She checked the date of the mail. It had been sent six days ago.

Heyy Babyy

Ritu sat in the waiting room at the hospital, flipping the pages of a three month old issue of *Femina*. She looked at her watch; it was an hour past her appointment. *Because it was called a waiting room, the doctors seemed to think they could make you wait as long as they liked.*

The room was softly lit and decorated in pastel shades. There was an aquarium in the corner where fishes swam sleepily, oblivious to the vociferous provocations of two boys outside. In front of her was a portrait of Mary with baby Jesus in her lap. Mary glanced at baby Jesus with an expression that was more 'Where did you come from?' than the beatific motherly look the painter was aiming for.

The room was full of pregnant women, suffering husbands and bratty children. Dr Bharati Pande was a leading gynaecologist of the city and seemed to command a committed following.

It wasn't easy, but in the end, she had decided to accept the London offer. Moving to London would mean Aayush attending The Royal Academy of Music in person. And that meant possibilities. Opportunities he never had before. They were to leave in a month's time. For one year. But if past assignments of this kind were any indication, her term could be extended.

And that decision had led her to being in the hospital. She had been undecided about her pregnancy, but once the move to London became certain, she knew what she had to do.

She had a consultation with Dr Pande in her clinic the week before. She was in the hospital for the procedure. *Procedure! Like it was a filing or documentation procedure!* It was simple, Dr Pande had explained. She would undergo a few tests and if everything was fine, Dr Pande would carry it out that day. She would have to stay overnight and go back home the following day.

She hadn't told either her parents or Sameer; she could handle this by herself.

Ritu hadn't told him about London either – she didn't have the heart. *Leaving at a time when he needs me the most.*

Sameer had taken the firing hard. His fragility had been a surprise; she had always thought of him as resilient. It was strange how certain events could trigger the worst in people. Stonewell had become a part of Sameer's identity and he felt adrift on losing that moor. She tried to talk him out of his anger, his resentment, but he couldn't seem to let go. He had been framed, she understood. But shit happened. And you move on.

She put down the *Femina* on the peg table beside her. There were a number of books lying there: *What to expect when you are expecting, Chicken soup for the expectant mother's soul, The first year, The pregnant body.*

Nothing on abortion.

Ritu didn't see him when he entered the room. In fact, she first noticed the strikingly beautiful woman he was with. A face that commanded attention; smiling dark eyes, silk hair, rosebud lips, high cheekbones, luminous skin. Shades of Katrina Kaif. She was young, in her mid-twenties perhaps, and wore a pale blue salwar kameez over her slim form.

Ritu noticed him only when the two of them sat right next to her. Even then, it was he who made the first move. He reached out to her. After a moment of hesitation, she reciprocated and held his outstretched hand. When their hands met, he smiled. All dimples. She fell for him right then and there.

She reached out with her other hand and touched his head with its wispy hair. He was a few months old, five or six perhaps. The feel of the soft skin and the baby powder smell transported her to the days when a six-month-old had bounced in her lap.

He let go of her finger, but extended his hand out to her again. She realized he was after her earrings, the shiny gold hoops. Ritu brought her ear closer to his outstretched hand. He got excited, rocked on his mother's lap, and played with the earring, slapping his hand on it. His mother smiled at Ritu and the origin of his dimples became clear.

Ritu beckoned to him, her arms outstretched. He came readily, risking the stranger for the pleasure of playing with the toys her ears were. The moment Ritu held him, she knew she was lost. His little body melded perfectly in hers, his toes brushed her arms as she felt the delicate skin of his cheek.

Ritu touched his nose and he burst out in a laughter that surprised her. She did it again and he gurgled even louder this time. Everyone in the room looked at them; smiling faces, anticipating more. She touched his nose again. To meet the expectations of people in the room. And he obliged with a no-holds-barred guffaw.

"Ritu Mathur!" Just then, the receptionist called out her name.

She froze.

"Ritu Mathur!" The receptionist, a young woman with eczema spots, called again.

Ritu didn't look directly at the receptionist, but sensed her gaze settling on her. With the full house in the waiting room, the receptionist wasn't sure who Ritu Mathur was, but had a vague idea it might be her.

The receptionist called out directly to her, "Madam, are you Ritu Mathur?"

She looked right into the eyes of the receptionist and shook her head. "No."

"Turn *aati hai to gayab. Ab* wait *karna padega toh* she'll complain," the receptionist whined, talking to no one in particular. Ritu nodded her head, silently joining her in her tirade against this Ritu Mathur, who had sneaked out right when the good doctor wanted to see her.

"Renuka Dhawan!" The receptionist moved on the next name on her list.

A very pregnant woman stood up, her husband extending his hand for support, and trudged into the doctor's room.

Ritu gave a resounding kiss on the cheek of the baby in her lap and handed him back to his mother.

Outside, it was a clear day. The roses in the hospital compound were in bloom and the bustle in the street beyond welcoming. Ritu closed her eyes and took a deep breath. *The world was beautiful.*

OMG Oh My God!

❋

The first time Tania saw her, she wasn't sure it was really her. They were on the adjacent escalators in the DLF Place mall in Saket. Tania was going up; she was coming down. Her face was turned away from Tania. The second time when Tania saw her, in *Fifth Avenue*, she was a few feet away. She seemed unaware of Tania, sifting through a rack of women's tops. Tania took cover behind the winter clothing rack, her heart racing, and watched the woman.

As Ritu left the store, Tania started to follow.

Shruti called out to Tania, *"Kahan?"*

"I have to go," Tania said, her eyes following Ritu.

"Dude, we just arrived…"

"I know."

Shruti looked at Tania's face, put back the two hangers she had in her hands and said, *"Chal."*

"You stay." She was out of the store before Shruti could protest any further. She looked around, afraid she had lost the woman. Then she spotted her on the right, by the bright pink turtle neck she wore. She was at an artificial jewellery stall, toying with a chunky pendant.

Tania stood at a nearby book stall, pretending to leaf through a magazine, watching her.

She paid up for a few pieces of jewellery. For a moment, Tania imagined her Dad's hands touching the pieces of jewellery on the woman's body. She felt nauseous.

She trailed the woman again, her temple throbbing. Tania saw her hesitate outside another store before she went in. Tania followed at a safe distance, beginning to realize the meaninglessness of this pursuit, but not quite ready to give it up. She was surprised to find herself amidst cute little outfits, complete with tiny caps and booties, cribs, toys, teethers, feeding bottles. *What was the woman doing there?*

She rushed out of the shop, her face flushed with anger.

It could be anything, she reasoned to herself. She could be buying things for a friend or a colleague who had a baby.

She waited for her outside the shop. The weekend shoppers ambled by. A young woman kneeled in front of her little son, wiping his face with a tissue, even as he made her job difficult by putting the ice cream cone in his hand to his nose again.

It was a while before Ritu stepped out of the store. Tania saw her holding two bags with the shop's sign on them. *Mama's Pet*. There seemed to be more purpose to the woman's steps now. She walked to the ground floor parking and got into her car. Tania sprinted towards the auto rickshaw stand outside the mall exit.

"*Bhaiya, woh red Alto ke peeche.*"

The driver – long hair, leather jacket and jeans with chains – flicked his hair. Tens of images of Salman Khan assailed her as she sat down. The young Prem of *Maine Pyaar Kiya* smiled at her from the back of the driver's seat rest, the six pack shirtless avatar looked down from the roof and Chulbul Pandeys from the two *Dabanggs* were to her sides. *A major fan.*

The auto rickshaw winded behind the car on the crowded Delhi roads, honking freely, most of the time for no reason. She thought of irrelevant things to avoid thinking of the ridiculousness of her chase. *Why had the autorickhaw driver hung a CD in the front? Did he think shiny discs were decorative? Were they Salman movies? Why were half the people on the road wearing brown sweaters? Was it like Delhi's winter colour? How many kids were in the van on her left? How did they get in the van - in the order of big to small? Why were all the TV sets in the electronic goods shop tuned to the same channel?*

It was five in the evening, but the sky had turned grey, the colour of the road. Grey above, grey below. A grey world with grey air.

She didn't know where the woman lived. They crossed the Chirag Delhi flyover, close to their home. For a strange second, she wondered if she was going there. But then her car went straight ahead. The chase continued.

She felt a raindrop on her cheek, as she paid up the auto rickshaw driver, who flicked his hair again in the Salman Khan style of *Tere Naam*. The woman got out of the car and climbed the stairs to her apartment. They were in Malviya Nagar. Tania felt foolish standing there alone in the rain and the cold, far from home.

She knew she should head back and give up this stupid adventure. But she couldn't. There was a reason she had come all this way. She had to know.

With a resolve fuelled by anger, Tania climbed the stairs to the woman's apartment and pressed the doorbell. There was some commotion inside, before an elderly woman draped in a sari opened the door, looking at her wet clothes. Tania realized she hadn't even thought of the possibility of other people being in the house.

"Ms Ritu?" Tania asked. She smelled frying onions.

"Second floor," the woman shot back, ostensibly used to people knocking on the wrong door.

She started to climb another flight of stairs. The sound of her shoes on the steps echoed in the silence of the stairwell. A gust of wind blew from a broken windowpane on the landing, making her shiver in her wet clothes. She paused when she reached the door of the apartment on the second floor. It was her last chance to turn back.

Her finger pressed the doorbell. The soft sound of the chime reached her from behind the closed doors. The house seemed quiet. She pressed the bell a second time, half hoping for the silence to continue. This time, the door opened, and she was face to face with her.

"Yes?" The woman peered at her for a moment before her face registered the surprised recognition. "Tania?"

Tania looked away.

"Come in," the woman said, stepping aside for her to get in.

"I don't want to." Tania's voice trembled, the words coming up unevenly. She shivered. "I want to know why you're doing this."

The woman seemed calm. "Won't it be better if you came inside?"

"No! I don't want to. Do you even know how you've ruined our lives? My mother's dead, my father unemployed. Why are you doing this?"

The woman stood there, looking shocked. She recovered quickly though. "If you meant to give me a piece of your mind, I believe you've done that and you can go home happy. But if you want to talk, I guess you'll have to come in first. We can't have this conversation standing here."

Tania didn't know why she went in. Maybe she really wanted to know. Maybe she was tired and cold and the inside looked warm.

It was a room designed to overwhelm the guest. Too much crammed in too little space. Furniture, photographs, paintings, curios everywhere. The wall besides the dining table was covered with masks. There was the Buddha in wood – sanguine and peaceful; a woman in porcelain – her lower face covered; an African one, long and dark, with gold trimmings on top and bottom. There was a ferocious looking one in the centre. Bulging wild eyes, sharp canines sticking out and life-like hair and moustache. *Why would you want something so hideous in your living room?*

She kept near the dining table, subconsciously staying close to the door. The woman went inside to what appeared to be a bedroom and handed her a towel. "You should dry yourself."

With some hesitation, she asked Tania, "Would you like a change of clothes? I can find you something that'll fit."

"No," Tania said, the idea of wearing the woman's clothes repugnant.

The woman looked at her and pointed to the sofa. "I'll get you a hot cup of tea – will warm you up."

"No, I don't want any."

The woman was gone. She called out from the kitchen, "It'll take a minute."

Tania sat there alone in the living room, confused. *What am I doing here? What will Dad say when he finds out about my adventure? What was I thinking?* Perhaps, that was the problem. When she got angry, she stopped thinking.

The woman came back in the room with two cups of tea and a plate of bourbon biscuits on a glass tray. She handed Tania a cup and put the biscuits on the table next to her.

She smiled. "You like those, don't you? Your Dad mentioned once—" she stopped mid-sentence, realizing her mistake in bringing him up.

She sat down on the sofa across from Tania and sipped from her cup. The cup of hot tea felt good in Tania's hand. It smelled of honey and ginger, her mother's cure for cold.

They sat in silence for a few moments. Tania's anger was waning.

The woman said softly, "What did you want to know so desperately that you came all the way here?"

Tania then thought of the question she most wanted to ask, "Are you pregnant?"

The woman all but dropped her cup, her composure evaporating. Whatever she had been expecting Tania to ask, it wasn't that.

"Oh my god, you are!" Tania put her cup down and it clanged against the glass of the table. She stood up, trembling again, "You are so… shameless."

"Watch yourself." The woman said, still sitting.

"Don't tell me what to do. You're not my mother."

"Sit down, Tania."

"I don't even know what I'm doing here." Tania started towards the door.

"*Sit down, Tania!*"

Despite herself, Tania sat down, still shaking her head in disbelief.

The woman seemed to have regained her poise. "I know I can't take your mother's place. I wouldn't even want to. I am content… being me."

"But are you pregnant?"

"I'd rather not talk about it."

It was then Tania noticed the half-hidden face peering at them from the bedroom. The boy. *So he had been home all along.* His presence made her conscious of her behaviour with his mother.

The woman followed her gaze to the boy.

She smiled at him. "Aayush, come here."

He shuffled along, his eyes on the ground, as if he was looking for something.

"This is Tania." The woman introduced them.

"Tania," he repeated, his eyes on her shoes.

Tania felt stifled in that cluttered room, in the presence of this strange pair of mother and son.

She got up again, "I should go."

"It's getting dark. Can I drop you?"

"No, I can go by myself."

"Are you sure? Aayush and I won't mind a ride…"

"No," she said abruptly. "If I can come here on my own, I can go back too."

Tania bolted out of the front door, bounding down the steps. She ran in one direction, without caring where she was going, oblivious to the rain and the cold. All she wanted to do was to get as far from that house as she could.

Koshish

It was eight in the morning. Sameer lay in bed, awake. *I should get up. Not that there was a reason to; there was nowhere to go.* It was strange, being at home, with no order to the day. Eating and sleeping all the time – his idea of a perfect vacation. But this wasn't much fun. He felt like a prisoner. Going out to the golf course wasn't an option either. The newspapers had made him much too famous.

There was a job interview the week before. With a family run pharma company in Okhla – the kind he would have never considered working for in the good days. However, yesterday, the head hunting agency had called to tell him the company had selected a guy ten years younger. At forty-three, he was considered too old for the position. If the Stonewell infamy didn't decimate his chances, the age did. He didn't feel old. Though he had to admit, when he was thirty, forty-three did seem over the hill.

Since the day of his firing, Anand has been helpful, doing all he could to help him find a suitable opening. Arun too. Sameer knew he had to wait for the right time; there had been too much in the press. In another six months or a year, people would get over it.

It would be great if he found a job that didn't demand too much of this time; the kids needed him much more than before. But for now, he would be happy to take whatever came his way.

There was this unspent, unexpressed anger with Ketan and Stonewell he couldn't shake off, however hard he tried. How could he have been so naïve? He did exactly what they wanted him to.

He sat cross-legged on the carpet, his eyes closed, trying to concentrate on his breath. *Breathe in, breathe out, and empty the mind of all thoughts.* Ritu's suggested remedy of getting over his anger. It was only a few minutes before Ketan snuck back into his thoughts. *This meditation business doesn't work for me.*

He ambled to the bathroom and peered at himself in the mirror. There were faint ageing lines from the edge of his lips to his chin, giving an impression of a permanent scowl. He pressed his cheeks back to make the lines disappear. His stubble was like a crop waiting to be harvested. He lathered his face and started to shave.

Money-wise, they were fine for some time. But if he didn't find a job in a few months, he may have to liquidate some of his investments. Those funds were meant for kids' education and his retirement. He hadn't counted on being unemployed.

As the comforting warm water of the shower washed down his body, he remembered it was Sunday. The kids were home. With Tania, it had been an on-off situation. There were times when she talked and then times when she clammed up. Like the dinner last week at her favourite restaurant *Diva*.

Sitting on the sofa across from him, under a black and white picture of the leaning tower, Pari had been chirping away as usual. "... and then Neel asked Archana ma'am – do you have a boyfriend. She was sooo mad..."

He made an attempt to draw Tania into the conversation. "What's happening in your class?"

"Usual."

He dabbed his mouth with the napkin in his lap. "How're your friends doing? Shruti, Aditi...haven't seen her for a while."

"Okay."

"Do you like your pasta?"

"Yes."

She remained like that the entire evening. Unresolved anger. Not unlike him.

Once, at home, he tried to talk to her about how she felt, but she left the room without answering. But he wasn't going to give up. Not this time. He stabbed a piece of watermelon with his fork and put it in his mouth. Perhaps that had been his mistake in the past, quitting too easily.

He heard Dayal come into the kitchen with grocery and a cheerful greeting. "Good morning, Ammaji!"

Ammaji grunted a response.

"Ammaji ka mood theek na hai – kal match haar gaye?"

Ammaji grumbled, *"Woh toh kambakht Ishant ne harwa diya.* He gave away fifteen runs in the last over."

"Galti toh Dhoni ki hai na. Kyon dalwaya last over Ishant *se*?" Dayal said.

"Hey Ram! Ab is mein bhi kasoor Dhoni ka? Muey Ishant ka nahin?"

Dayal chuckled in satisfaction.

"Arey, Dhoni nahin hota, toh cup bhi nahin milta. Captain Cool *aise hi nahin bolte.* You don't understand a thing."

Dayal roared with laughter; baiting Ammaji was his favourite sport. Ammaji was from Jharkhand and could not endure a word against her state's hero.

Sameer was glancing at the headlines in the newspaper when he felt Pari's soft arms around his neck. "Barefoot again? Get your slippers."

Pari didn't make any move to let go of him; he didn't want her to either. Her breath was mouthwash minty.

Ammaji cleared the dishes and asked, *"Aaj lunch kya banega?"* Her magenta shirt claimed she was 'America's next supermodel'.

This was the decision making he did these days – what was to be cooked. The ex-Assistant Financial Controller of Stonewell. Not that it mattered – everything Ammaji made tasted about the same. She was an efficient cook, but by no means imaginative. Her chicken curry and *aloo matar* had the same ingredients (except of course chicken and *aloo matar*), were cooked the same way, and ended up tasting the same too. Kavita didn't cook often, but she varied the menu, supervised Ammaji in the kitchen, and experimented with new dishes. The meals weren't boring then.

"Black daal?" He whispered to Pari for her approval.

"Boring." She pouted.

They could go out, but he didn't know if Tania would want to. The night before, she had come back late in the evening. In a pretty bad mood too. Straight to her room. No dinner.

Then it occurred to him. "I know what we can do."

Pari came around and sat in the chair across from him, a smile on her lips, her eyes expectant.

He put the newspaper down and looked at her. Her hair shone as a tiny ray caught her head. "Let's give Ammaji a break. *We* will make lunch today. Tania, you and me."

He wasn't an accomplished cook. Far from it. But he was, as he called himself, *an internet cook*. Years before, when they didn't have Ammaji's services, he made dinner every Sunday. It was meant to be a break for Kavita. When Tania was four or so, she had joined in, and it became a father-daughter activity. One of the fondest memories he had of little Tania was her following him around; asking him what ingredient he needed next, stirring, tasting, giving opinions; the complicity in crime when they substituted an ingredient or when things got out of hand; the suspense when they put the dish on the table and waited for Kavita's reaction.

Then somewhere along the line, it stopped. Work. Golf. Ammaji. First, it became those Sundays when he could, and then he halted altogether.

Pari looked at him, puzzled. The sun was in her eyes now and she shielded them with her hands. "Why?"

He stretched his arms and pulled her cheeks. "Because it's fun."

Pari wasn't convinced, he could see.

He searched for recipes online and then remembered. There was this one dish Tania particularly liked. Green chicken, she called it. He searched by the key ingredients. There it was. *Chicken in pistachio, cilantro pesto. Italian.*

"What do you think?" He asked Pari, showing her the picture.

"Looks yummy," she said.

He scanned through the ingredients list and checked with Ammaji. They had everything except fresh cilantro and lemons.

He ruffled Pari's hair. "Ask Tania to get ready. I'll fetch the raw materials for our project!"

"Aye, aye, captain."

He stepped out to a sunny winter day and took delight in the warmth of the sun on his limbs. Sameer loved Delhi winters. He could laze around on the balcony, all day long, basking in the sun. The season of roasted peanuts, carrot juice and *moong dal ka halwa*. Couldn't get better than that.

The park outside their home was alive with activity. The children's corner with swings, slides and monkey bars, was busy. A sniffling small boy spun the merry go around for his friends, faster and faster, and then jumped on it with a whoop.

Keshav played cricket with his ten-year-old son in his front yard. They were both dressed in the light blue Team India jerseys. Sameer stopped the car in front of their house and waved to him. Payal and Keshav had been a rock of support these last few months.

"Where to?" Keshav asked with the cricket bat tucked under his arm.

"Market. Kids and I are making lunch today."

Keshav smiled under his baseball cap. "I should come over then."

"Payal ji cooks innovative dishes for you every day—"

"Exactly. Wish someone would tell her she can't cook. God knows, I don't have the courage." Keshav pushed up his thick glasses.

Sameer laughed.

"For the last twelve years, she has packed me lunch every day and I have handed it over to one beggar or another. *Ab toh,* even beggars have stopped accepting – *nahin sahib, nahin chahiye.*" Keshav laughed.

Just then, Payal stepped out of the house and shouted, "Sameer ji, I have made some vegetarian lasagna with whole wheat pasta. Please take some."

Keshav shouted back, "They're going out for lunch." He winked at Sameer. "You owe me one."

Sameer laughed as he drove. *Poor Keshav. To be subjected to Payal's cooking every day.*

At the traffic signal, Imran was at his window as soon as he stopped, flashing his white smile. When he lowered the windowpane, Imran waved a magazine at him. *"New Women's Era,* sir."

He smiled, took it from him and reached for his wallet. With a start, he remembered that the reader of the magazine was gone. He bought it anyway.

Pari was absorbed in TV when he got back home. No sign of Tania.

"She's busy. She has a test tomorrow," Pari explained.

Again.

"Did you tell her what we're cooking?"

"I showed her the recipe." Pari's fingers made a rectangle in air.

Even though not surprised, he was disappointed. He considered talking to her, but wasn't sure if he should right then. Kavita would have known what to do; when to intervene and when to give her space.

"So are we cooking or not?" Pari asked, interrupting his thoughts.

"Of course, we are." He smiled at her. "In fact, today is the first day of your training to be the Junior Master Chef."

She beamed back at him. "Yeah! Get out of the way Nitika Gandhi. Pari Chadha is here!" Nitika was the winner of the last season.

They looked for Kavita's cooking aprons and found two with patterns of forks and knives on them. Pleased at her professional appearance, Pari took a selfie of both of them in their identical apparel.

He asked Pari to shell the pistachios. She ate more than she saved; it was sometime before they had enough. He stuck them in the oven. By the time, the warm, festive aroma of roasted pistachios wafted into the kitchen, they had the rest of the ingredients ready on the kitchen counter. The cilantro leaves and garlic had been chopped (Pari allowed the knife for the first time ever – for about thirty seconds before he got scared and took it away), the lemon juice squeezed, the cardamom ground.

Everything got in the blender and they had the green paste. He remembered how Tania loved the next step, which was to pack the sauce inside the loosened skin of chicken breasts. She loved getting her hands dirty. He wondered if Pari would like it too. She loved it. She laughed, as her fingers got all sticky.

He slid the chicken into the oven and set the timer. They watched *Sponge Bob Square Pants* in their break.

Still no sign of Tania.

The aroma of grilled chicken began to fill the room. When the timer sounded, he took the chicken out. Pari arranged the chicken on a serving dish and drizzled the remaining sauce on it.

"Ta da!" Pari displayed the final product to him with a flourish.

"Great job, Chef Pari."

She curtsied.

"Call Tania."

She came back alone. "She's not hungry."

That got him. He stood up in a huff, but then checked himself. *Patience.*

One end of the Justin Bieber poster on the wall had come lose and was curling. Her bed was still unmade and she wore the previous day's clothes. Tania was on her desk, her body taut with tension. She didn't look up when he came and stood by the door. "Hey."

No answer.

"Why're you not eating?"

"Why does anyone not eat? I'm not hungry," she said, eyes still on the book on the desk.

"I… we have made green chicken. You remember how you loved to cook with me, getting your hands all green—"

"Of course I remember, Dad. I remember everything. I am surprised you do, considering…"

"What?"

She lifted her eyes and looked at him. "Considering you're starting a brand new family – new wife, new baby."

Kabhi Alvida Na Kehna

The doorbell rang as Ritu washed the dishes after dinner. Leaving the plates in the sink, her hands wet and soapy, she hurried to open the door.

She smiled at him. "Look who's here."

Sameer stepped inside with his lopsided smile.

"Where's Aayush?" he asked after her, as she went back to the kitchen.

"At my parents' place. Lohri celebrations in the colony," she shouted over the sound of water rinsing her hands.

She came back and sat next to him. This was the first time Sameer had come home since Kavita's death. He seemed to have lost some weight; he looked fit in a wine-red pullover and dark trousers.

There was strangeness between them, as they sat stiffly, their limbs not touching. His eyes were on an addition to the wall of masks. A brass mask of the Sun God, little rays sticking out of a serene round face. She followed his eyes and smiled. "Neena brought it from Orissa."

The conversation was bumpy; awkward silences, laboured starts. The unseasonably cold weather, Aayush's upcoming performance, her father's health, Pari's school. She had this habit of filling periods of silence and kept on doing so till she ran out of topics.

Finally, he asked, "What've you decided about your pregnancy?"

Pregnancy. Not baby. He doesn't see the baby. I do.

The question hung in the air. The sound of a door banging somewhere punctuated the silence of the room. She looked at him. "You don't have to feel responsible for the baby. There's so much going on with you."

Holding her hand, he said, "I want to know. It concerns both of us, doesn't it?"

His hand felt warm. "I've decided to keep the baby." She looked at his face, searching for a reaction.

She was a little surprised by what she found. Acceptance.

Ritu felt a joy deep within her. A contentment that didn't need words. They sat in silence, their fingers intertwined.

It was a while before Sameer spoke again. "Can I ask you something?" Kissing the palm of her hand, he said, "Will you marry me, Ritu?"

She thought of the many times the scene had played out in her mind. His asking the question, her flinging her arms around his neck, kissing him in ecstasy and saying – "Yes, of course, I will marry you!" as Beethoven's fifth symphony played in the background.

But reality was different.

"Why do you want to marry me, Sameer?" she asked softly.

"Because it's the right thing to do."

"That, I'm afraid, wasn't the answer I was looking for." She smiled.

He protested, "But I…"

"Don't say anything you're not sure about, Sameer." Her fingers played with the tiny hair on the back of his hand. "You know what has been the best thing about our relationship? Honesty. At no point of time, you led me on, or I you. Let's not ruin this by entering a realm of which we know little."

She leaned back on the sofa. "After being in a decaying marriage for long, I'd want to marry again for the right reason. And the right reason has to come from here." She touched her chest. "I'll marry when I'm loved unconditionally, wanted for who I am, with all my faults and failings. Perhaps I will be loved like that one day. Perhaps not. But I'll not marry because the world expects me to... *because it's the right thing to do."*

He was quiet, the room silent except for the buzz of the tube light. She heard the chipper tweet of a car being unlocked and then the engine coming to life in the street below.

He said, "There's a baby on the way and he or she needs a father. So does Aayush. I'm not saying it'll be easy – the kids living together, but it does seem the best way."

She was pleased to hear him say baby for the first time. She said, "Maybe," twirling the silver ring on her finger, "But if I accepted today, I'd always believe you married me because of the baby, not because you wanted to. And I can't live with that."

"But—"

She put her hand on his cheek. "There's one more thing I need to tell you." She told him about London – the job offer, Aayush's admission, and her decision to leave.

He looked shocked. "When were you planning to tell me? If you meant to tell me at all?"

"Don't be silly." She squeezed his hand. "How could I have left without telling you? But there's so much going on in your life... I couldn't bring myself to add more."

"Why?"

Her feet were cold and she rubbed them on the Kashmiri rug underneath the glass coffee table. "You know why, Sameer. I can't deny Aayush the opportunity." She looked away from him.

He was quiet again. She knew it was a difficult argument to refute.

"How'll you manage with Aayush and the baby?"

"My practical Sameer." She smiled at him. "I'll figure it out. Aayush will stay with his grandparents till I set up home in London.

My parents may join us for some time to help with the baby. We'll find a way."

"And what will I do without you?"

Her arms wrapped him in a sideways hug and she rested her head on his shoulder. "You'll be fine. You have to take care of your daughters," she said. She looked at him. "Besides, it's only for a year."

She laid her head back on his shoulder. The texture of his pullover against her cheek was soft. "...who knows how we'll feel after one year. The distance may make the hearts grow fonder as they say... or we may find what we have between us isn't enough. But I'll always be there for you and I know you'll be for me – that's something..."

She pulled his face towards her and kissed him on the lips. He responded, but when the kissing got passionate, he withdrew. They hadn't made love since that fateful evening.

She whispered, "It's okay."

They made love there in the living room. Slowly, lingeringly. The masks and the dolls watching them. She savoured each moment, squirreling it away in her mind. She wanted to remember each touch, each caress, each kiss. The feel of his hand and lips on her body, his warm breath against hers, the moistness of his tongue on her breasts, the lemony fragrance of his cologne behind his ear, the feel of her flesh pressed against his, the familiar sensation of fulfillment when he entered her, the smile in his eyes when she came, his slowing down to allow her to savour her moment, and then seeing him close his eyes when he came. It was beautiful. As always. She wanted to capture everything. It might be the last time that magic happened.

Afterwards, they lay together in the bedroom, snug under the blanket, her head on his chest, his arms around her. Her eyes closed; she loved these moments of repose, culmination.

She woke up to his kiss.

"I have to go..." he said.

She looked at the wall clock across from the bed. It was ten. Sitting propped by pillows, she watched him dress and started to panic. She jumped up from the bed and wrapped her arms around him, naked in the cold room.

Sameer was almost dressed, when she said, "Wait."

Shivering in the cold, she put on her nightgown, opened the cupboard across the bed and took out a gift wrapped package. "For you."

Sameer smiled and started to open the ribbon when she held his hand. "Not now. After I'm gone."

When they kissed in the living room, they lingered a long time, before she opened the door to let him out. She stood in the chill, looking at him go.

Uphaar

Sameer tied the shoe laces of his sneakers and ran down the steps. The park was relatively quiet. No children on the swings; it was a school day. A group of elderly men argued politics, sitting together on a cluster of wooden benches. Jogging on the walking track that weaved its way through the park, Sameer waved to the bald guy with the A.K. Hangal look he saw often.

Some of the flowers were in bloom; the scent of spring in the air. The Sweet-Williams flowerbed was vibrant with colours – purple, magenta, white, red – in a mad collision. He passed a patch of rose bush, where delicate pink buds of roses had started to appear.

A woman, with a baby in her arms, entered the park through the turnstile. From her appearance, an immigrant laborer, who probably worked on one of those construction sites that were springing up everywhere. With names like Malibu Town, Avalon Gardens, and Kasablanca Towers, hoardings that showed lush green grass and blue skies, you would think they were advertising properties in Switzerland or Canada.

He was beginning to sweat; his T-shirt clung to his back. Perhaps he should shift his jogging to the evenings or early mornings. It was getting warmer. He smiled at the thought. *I am getting too used to my leisurely ways. Of having the entire day to myself.*

The woman sat cross-legged on the grass and laid out a cloth for the infant to lie on. The baby gurgled, reaching for a plastic duck the mother held in her hand.

He watched their interaction from a distance, sitting in the shade of a gulmohar tree, its dark brown pods strewn about on the ground below. A breeze cooled his sweat.

He chuckled as the little one let out a spout of water, taking the woman by surprise. *A boy.* The mother mock admonished the son as she changed his nappy.

His thoughts drifted to the yet-to-be-born baby. Ritu had left for London the week before. He wondered how he would feel when the child arrived. Would he not want to see his kid? What if Ritu stayed in London long term and raised the baby there? Would the baby know him as the father? A sharp prick on his fingertip alerted him to ants marching in a straight line across his hand. Apparently he had become a part of their route. He got up and brushed them off.

It would be Ritu's prerogative to decide, what role, if any, he has in the baby's growing up. Maybe he would get periodic packages in the mail. Baby updates.

The thought of a package reminded him of Ritu's gift. He had forgotten about it. He decided to return home.

He looked over the jasmine shrub in the balcony. With the onset of spring, it seemed to be coming back to life. The leaves had a luster to them and there was a hint of flower buds. He smiled. His nurturing over the last few months seemed to be paying off. He watered them using Kavita's can. In the sun, the water drops looked like little rainbows falling and disappearing in the earth.

"*Nimboo paani*, Ammaji!" He called out after a quick shower and took the package out of the bedroom closet. It was a small packet bound in a wrapping paper with patterns of tiny Russian dolls, tied with a white ribbon. He loosened the string and tore open the packaging. There were two CDs in slim cases with no labels. He smiled. This was a bit teen-ish of her. Making him CDs. But then they did have a shared interest in music. Bollywood songs of 70s and 80s. Walking into the living room, he stuck one in the CD player. He reclined on the sofa, took a sip of the lemonade and waited for the music.

Nothing happened. He got up to check. The sun-drenched floor felt warm to his bare feet.

The music system showed an error. *Disc not compatible.* He tried the second. Same result. He cleaned the disc's surface with a soft cloth and put it back in.

Nothing.

Maybe it's the CD player. He gulped the remaining lemonade in his glass, relishing the cold burst of tanginess in his mouth, and walked to the bedroom. After the brightly lit living room, it took him a minute to adjust to the darkness there. He inserted the first CD in his laptop. It's when he opened the first folder, he understood why the CD player hadn't played the music.

It was not a music CD. It was a data CD.

He stared baffled at the screen displaying a list of folders.

The first file he opened was an e-mail, from Ketan to Kartik, asking for Stonewell's financial statements to be signed on a particular date.

His curiosity aroused, he scanned through the other files.

He was stunned. E-mails. A hundred or so. From Ketan's account.

Sorting them by date, from the oldest to the most recent, Sameer started reading. For the next three hours, he was riveted to the computer. Ammaji came in to ask if he wanted lunch, but he waved her away and told her to shut the door behind her.

When he finished reading the last e-mail, he leant back in the chair, his hands behind his head, still grasping the gravity of what he had just read.

Ritu had somehow managed to pull out confidential mails from Ketan's e-mail account, that when read together, told the complete story of Stonewell's financial statements scam. He was astonished by how well-planned the whole racket was.

It was Ketan's idea. The profitability of the pharmaceutical sector was under pressure and Stonewell's financial statements for the last two quarters hadn't been promising. The company needed to raise money for the new vaccine plant and hence the public issue. Ketan had pitched the idea of adding Biochem numbers to Srini, the CEO, for the March quarterly reports, even though Biochem had become a Stonewell subsidiary only in May. Then they had discussed it with some of the Board members individually, ones they thought they could win over. Bansal, the Finance Director, had backed them. He remembered Bansal from the Board meeting, all fire and brimstone. "My recommendation is to discharge Mr Chadha from his current responsibilities as his malicious and ill-informed conduct has cost the company its peerless reputation."

Ketan had indicated he'd ask the Finance department to do the first numbers and had picked Kartik for the job. He had then covered his tracks by being out of the country when the financial statements were to be signed. Nitin was sent to London on training. And Sameer had conveniently ended up being the fall guy.

Things soured, however, when Nikhil Roy's article came out.

There was some finger pointing initially between Board members, Srini and Ketan. But then there was talk of damage control and an understanding was reached to wash their hands off the whole issue and let Sameer take the hit.

The mails were not direct; each mail in itself wasn't potent. However, if you read the entire thread, the story was clear enough.

Ketan was no fool, to keep every piece of the plot documented that could incriminate him later. He had done it to protect his own ass. There was a note from Bansal to Ketan when the *Financial Times* story broke out:

Dear Ketan,

It is really unfortunate that management has botched the public issue. In the best traditions of executive accountability, I suggest you resign, taking moral responsibility for the turmoil the company faces. The Board will protect and support you against any legal or regulatory action.

Ravi

Ketan's response was brief:

Dear Mr Bansal,

We swim or sink together. The Board and management worked together on the public issue (I have many pieces of evidence including our e-mail communication on the subject). I hope you understand.

Ketan

There was more.

Even though it had started out as a ploy to raise funds for the company, somewhere along the line, they had recognized the opportunity of making a neat bundle for themselves on the stock market when the much higher profits were reported. Ketan, Srini, Bansal and a few other Board members who were in it had bought substantial quantity of shares just before the publication of results. "You should be glad we are letting you off easy, not pressing charges for personal financial gains in the stock market."

There was an angry note from one of the Board members, Gautam Bhatia, to Ketan, at the time of Nikhil Roy's story breaking out, chiding Ketan for mismanagement. Bhatia hadn't been able to unload his shares.

Bhatia hadn't made money. But the others did. Apparently tons of it. This gave the whole game a new dimension. *Insider trading.* It wasn't any longer just the crime of inflating the financial statements of a company before a public issue. It was doing it deliberately to make money.

The plan seemed a purely India-centric one. There didn't seem any ostensible involvement of the London office. *Now I know who to report this to.*

How did Ritu get these documents? Ketan must have guarded them with his life. It was such a big risk too. Those guys could've gone any length to protect themselves. *That's why she asked me to open the gift after she was gone.*

She did it for him. She knew he had been unable to get over Stonewell. That he needed closure.

He looked at his watch. Three in the afternoon. Eleven in the morning in London. She would be at work. He called Stonewell's London office. An unknown classical piece, easy on the ears, played on the phone, as the call was transferred.

"Ritu," she said her name in her work-voice.

"Thank you… for the gift."

"Liked it?" He could hear the excitement in her voice.

"How did you…?"

"Long story."

"Dangerous though. Those guys—"

"Nothing happened. And I am thousands of miles away now," Ritu said, "I had help."

"Who?"

"Ashok. He had a friend in building management company. That's how I got the spare keys to Ketan's cabinets. Wasn't easy."

Ritu had to leave for a meeting and he hung up after a few minutes.

I should send the mails to the London office. They'd do what was necessary. I would be vindicated.

A thought occurred to him and he smiled. He got up, stretched and dialled a number on his cell.

"Nikhil Roy." The baritone voice on the other side was crisp and professional.

"Mr Roy, this is Sameer Chadha. Wonder if you remember me. I worked in Stonewell."

"Mr Chadha, what a surprise!" Roy said, clearly startled by Sameer's phone call, "What can I do for you?"

"I have something that would interest you."

Jaane Bhi Do Yaron

Harmeet tucked the dripping golgappa in his mouth, closed his eyes to savour its taste before pronouncing his verdict, "Umm… not quite Ludhiana, but, pass."

Tania smiled. "Thank you ji. You liked it – *hamari* life *ka* mission complete *ho gaya*." She didn't comment on the Ludhiana bit. In Harmeet's world, nothing in Delhi ever came close to Ludhiana.

Harmeet and Ishmit had been in Delhi for a week. Harmeet kept everyone in splits all day long. Ishmit, forever in his brother's shadow, tried hard too, but didn't always succeed. He made them laugh more at his failed attempts at humour than the jokes he told.

'What's the difference between a fly and a mosquito? A fly can fly but a mosquito can't mosquito. What's red and goes tring tring? A tomato. Tring tring was just to confuse you.'

And Harmeet liked to eat. Food was the number one topic of discussion every day. *Where would be lunch today? What does Ammaji make the best? Where do you get the best chhole-bhature in the city?*

That day, she had brought Harmeet to M block market in GK I; Ishmit and Pari choosing to stay back home. It was a weekday morning and the market wasn't too crowded. Besides a chubby girl in a printed dress about Pari's age, who was on to her third plate – they'd both admired her eating skills – they were the only customers at the shop.

The girl put another one in her mouth and her plump cheeks became plumper before she bit it and it dissolved in her mouth without spilling.

"You go, girl!" Harmeet patted the girl on her head. She eyed him suspiciously.

He turned to Tania. "*But tum Delhi waale ajeeb ho. Golgappe mein* mineral water? *Yaar, golgappe mein jab tak thoda gutter ka paani nahin hoga,* how will it taste good?"

Tania almost choked on the golgappa in her mouth, its piquant tartness hitting the back of her throat. She covered her mouth to avoid a mess and punched him on his arm.

"Where're we going for dinner today?" Harmeet asked while pointing to the vendor his empty plastic bowl, signalling for another one.

"*Bhukkad! Abhi yeh to kha le.*"

"*Golgappon se pet thode hi na bharta hai.*"

As they walked past the exquisite displays of Hazoorilal Jewelers on their way back, he said, arching his eyebrows, "*Aaj Mamaji ko phasate hain.* We should go to a really expensive place."

The idea of a dinner with her dad didn't sound too appetizing to Tania. She thought of a counter-plan. "You wanted to go dancing…"

"Where?"

"The best place in Delhi." She laughed. "That, dude, I promise you, will be better than Ludhiana."

Tania stood in front of the mirror, wearing the dress Mom had bought for her Grade Ten graduation party. Deep blue, double shade satin with a darker trim that ended a little above her knees. She had put on light make up – lip gloss and eye liner.

The doorbell chimed. Avantika had come to pick them up; her Dad was a member of Dublin in Maurya and had agreed to let them into the nightclub tonight. He was going to drive Harmeet, Avantika and Tania there. Pari and Ishmit had grudgingly accepted that they couldn't pass for eighteen.

"Harmeet, *chal*," she shouted.

He came out of Pari's room, which the two brothers had taken over, looking rather cool, in an open neck striped purple shirt, a matching turban and black trousers.

"Dashing?" he asked, posing in profile, hands on hips.

"LOL."

Ammaji was in the kitchen and Tania smelled cookies being baked, Pari's compensation for not going out. Tania called out to Ammaji, "We're leaving."

The doorbell rang again. As they hurried through the living room, she saw Dad coming out of his bedroom to get the door. He looked at them. "Where're you going?"

"Dancing." She looked at the door.

"You didn't think you needed to tell me?"

"I told Ammaji."

"You have to ask *me* if you're going out."

Harmeet first looked at her, then at her Dad. He seemed surprised she hadn't spoken to Dad about their plans for the evening.

Ding Dong.

"Avantika's waiting. We'll be late." She turned to go.

"Tania…"

She was out of the door before he could say anything further.

She heard Harmeet's conciliatory tone from outside the door, "*Mamaji…main jaaoon?*"

Bounding down the steps two at a time, her heart thudded. Harmeet followed.

"Were you sleeping?" Avantika whined, standing at the foot of the staircase, wearing an off-shoulder red dress Tania hadn't seen before, looking gorgeous as usual.

Introductions made, they got into the car and Avantika's Dad drove towards Chanakyapuri. Mehdi Hassan played on the car's music system and Harmeet felt the urge to have a conversation with Avantika's Dad.

"Uncle ji, can you follow all the verses? *Mujhe toh samajh hi nahin aata.* What does *marasim* mean? Why do they use such difficult language?"

"Why do they repeat each line four times? *Befkoof Samajhte hain hum ko? Chalo, meri akal toh zara chhoti hai.* But you understand all the lyrics…"

"Do you like Jagjit Singh, uncle ji? I think he was the best. I'm not saying it because he was a sikh…"

Tania thought of the scene at home. Perhaps she shouldn't have left like that. *Too late.*

"What time should I pick you guys up?" Avantika's Dad asked when he signed them into Dublin.

"I'll call you, Daddy," Avantika said.

"No later than twelve. Otherwise I'll bring your Mom. We'll both dance in the Bollywood style of the seventies and embarrass you."

"Yeah, yeah." Avantika kissed him on his cheek.

Tania smiled, imagining Avantika's parents dancing with them.

When Avantika went to the washroom and they were alone at their table, Harmeet frowned at her. "You didn't even ask Mamaji…"

She shrugged nonchalantly.

"Tu bhi yaar… marwaayegi." He shook his head.

As the music changed to a Lady Gaga song, she turned to look towards the dance floor. Her heart rate registered an acceleration as she spotted him among the crowd. Dressed simply in a white shirt and blue jeans, yet looking incredibly handsome, was Dhruv. He danced elegantly, at ease. The next moment she noticed Aditi dancing with him and the music started to jar. *Why does she always have to be with him?*

Avantika was back. "Let's go!"

"You guys go. I'll join later," Tania said.

"*Oye, chal na.*" Harmeet grabbed her hand and they made their way to the dance floor. It was already full, boys and girls in groups of twos and threes, with a few uncle-aunty couples shaking it too. It smelt of cologne and sweat. Harmeet and Avantika were both excellent dancers, they soon started moving to the rhythm of the techno music being played. Tania danced like she always did – self-conscious and stilted in her moves. A starved looking *firang*, his orange hair in beads, arms blue with tattoos, attempted to join their party, but was brushed off by Harmeet.

There was a tap on her shoulder and she turned to look at Dhruv smiling in the laser lights, "May I?"

Avantika winked at her as Tania turned to dance with Dhruv. Aditi was nowhere in sight.

Miley Cyrus sang about a wrecking ball and Tania felt like one herself; she had never danced worse. Her movements felt wooden. The song changed to a Bollywood favourite and Dhruv mimicked the moves from the movie. He was good – nimble and fluid in his movements. She tried to follow his lead, but her steps felt laboured. He noticed her discomfiture and held her hands to coordinate their moves. That didn't work too well either.

"Let's take a break," he said in her ear over the loud music, "I'm thirsty."

They found two empty places. The polished wooden top of the bar gleamed in the soft lights above.

"I'm such a crappy dancer," Tania apologized, climbing the stool.

He smiled at her. "You're alright. You just need to loosen up a bit." Beads of sweat glistened on his forehead.

"What can I get you?" He asked her as the barman approached them. A short guy with chinky eyes and spiky hair.

Dhruv checked with her and then ordered a Sprite for her and a beer for himself. She wondered if the barman would ask for an ID card for his beer. He didn't. He barely looked twenty-one himself.

Aditi joined them a little later. "What're you drinking?" Without waiting for an answer she took a gulp from Dhruv's glass and made a face, "Too strong."

"And what do you have?" Aditi asked her.

Tania picked up her glass lest Aditi sampled hers too, "Sprite."

"Sprite!" she shrieked. "You're such a good girl. Your parents must be so proud of you."

The reference to the plural stung her.

Aditi continued, without a care in the world, "Dhruv, *you* don't spoil her. Okay?"

Why the hell am I being a good girl? For who?

"I don't mind a glass of wine," she said, turning to Dhruv.

Aditi smirked, but held her tongue.

When her drink arrived, she picked up the glass, took a sip, and rolled it over her tongue. She had seen people tasting wine on TV. It was rancid, bitter. She gulped it down and her throat burned.

"Not bad," she pronounced.

Harmeet and Avantika joined them. Avantika was sweating; the high-energy dancing had taken its toll on her. However, Harmeet looked as fresh as he was when they came in. He looked at her drink, but didn't say anything. She'd almost finished with her glass, but didn't feel any different. *So much for the mystery of alcohol. One more disappointment with the adult world.*

"Boys and girls," DJ Sunny announced over the PA system, "here's one from the land of bhangra!" Amidst cheers of approval from the crowd, he played *London thumakda*. Harmeet's shoulders started going up and down almost involuntarily. He got up and extended a hand to Avantika, who folded her hands in response. He looked at Tania, but she refused too. He turned to Aditi, "Aditi!"

"Me? No!"

"What the fuck…" Aditi muttered, as she found herself dragged to the dance floor.

They watched in amusement, as Harmeet urged and then got Aditi to follow his moves.

When Dhruv and Tania made their way to dance floor again, she had finished her second glass and felt cheerful. When she danced, she was less inhibited than before. Her legs felt lighter, freer.

It was a little later that the alcohol really kicked in. As she got up to go the bathroom, she felt dizzy and sat back. Avantika steadied her as they headed to the bathroom together, but she noticed the sneer on Aditi's face.

Harmeet and Avantika decided it was time to go home. Given Tania's state, Avantika didn't want to call her Dad. Dhruv offered to drive them, but they declined; they took a taxi instead. By the time they reached home, she was really woozy and her temples pulsed. Fenced between Avantika and Harmeet, as she climbed the steps, she sort of floated in the air.

Dad was at the door even before they pressed the doorbell.

She expected him to shout at her when they were alone, as Harmeet went off to drop Avantika. But he didn't. When she retched for the first time, he was at her side, holding her shoulders and stroking her back, as she bent over the toilet.

"Have you eaten?" he asked when he settled her back in bed.

She shook her head.

He went out and came back with a sandwich, a glass of water and a pill. She didn't feel like eating, but chewed on the sandwich anyway. She recognized the medicine. *Avomine.* She used to take it for motion sickness as a child.

She threw up once more and he was there again. Afterwards, she fell into a fitful sleep, waking up with a parched throat at three in the morning to find a glass of water by her bedside. She dozed off again and dreamt she was a ballerina playing the lead in *Swan Lake*. Dhruv was in the audience, applauding her flawless performance.

It was nearly eleven in the morning when she woke up. A tiny person sat inside her head, using a hammer to break out. Her tongue was glued to the inside of her mouth. She found an aspirin and a fresh glass of water by her bedside. Dad seemed to anticipate her needs exactly.

She was still lounging in the bed, when there was a knock on the door. She braced herself for the storm that was overdue.

But it was Harmeet. "Good afternoon ji."

He grinned as he plopped himself on the chair next to her bed. "How're you feeling? *Tune toh kal had kar di yaar. Full talli!*"

She wasn't amused. "Is Dad very angry?"

"Surprisingly not as much as I would have thought. *Mere Dad ne toh laga diye hote do chaar abhi tak.*"

Surprising indeed. She hadn't known him to control his anger. "Is he home?"

"He was up all night, hovering around you. But he went out for a meeting an hour ago," Harmeet said. "*Chup chaap sorry bol dena. Lecture sun lena.* It'll be alright."

The mention of an apology rekindled the anger in her. "I don't know who should say sorry to whom."

Harmeet's smile waned as his eyes settled on her face, "*Jaane bhi de,* Tania. He didn't kill your Mom. Get over it."

Hip Hip Hurray

❀

Sameer checked the rearview mirror; the black Scorpio was still there. It was the same car which followed the girls and him back from their dinner the day before. From Moolchand flyover, he turned back and headed home. *It may not be safe to see Nikhil Roy today.*

The road in front of the house had a just swept look. Parking the car in the porch, he ran up the steps. Ammaji opened the door for him. The house was quiet. *Too quiet.*

"Where're the girls?"

"Woh Tania toh…"

"What?"

"Balcony." His urgency seemed to make Ammaji nervous.

"Pari?"

"Apne room mein hogi."

She wasn't. He rushed to check the other rooms. Not there.

Had she gone to the park? He had told her to stay indoors. He bounded down the steps. The Scorpio had followed him home; these men could be vile. He was on the halfway landing when he heard Pari's voice, "Dad!"

She was upstairs, in a lilac frock, beaming at him.

"Where were you?"

"Bathroom. Why?"

He held the banister and took a long breath.

The last few weeks had seen the biggest commotion in the Indian corporate world since Kingfisher. Nikhil Roy used the information on CDs strategically. After Roy reviewed the information, *Financial News* carried a story on the front page the next day, hinting the Stonewell management may have been involved in the financial statements fraud. The news immediately caught the attention of the business universe. As expected, the following day, Stonewell Board came back with a denial.

A few days later, Roy published the second installment, providing some details – names, dates, e-mails. That caused a buzz. A number of non-business newspapers were also drawn to the story. Gokhale, Chairman of Stonewell Board, announced the following day that Stonewell would investigate.

Sameer had been afraid for the safety of his family. Even though Nikhil Roy was careful and there wasn't been any indication of Sameer being the source, it was clear an insider was involved.

He walked over to the balcony. The fragrance of jasmine reached him before he saw them; they were in full bloom. Tiny white pearls amongst glistening green leaves. Tania fingered a bud, feet bare, hair open and a smile on her face. She looked up when she saw him, still smiling. "Mom had planted it just before she passed away. I thought the shrub was dying."

He smiled back and put an arm around her shoulder.

The Scorpio was parked a few houses down the lane, two men sitting in the front. The driver wore a khaki uniform, his companion was in a black jacket and dark glasses.

He said, "Let's go in."

"But…"

He ignored her protests, slid the glass doors shut and drew the curtains. Tania looked at him for an explanation, but he didn't offer any.

He called Roy.

"Take care. No need to take unnecessary risks," Roy said. "Wait till tomorrow."

The third and final installment. *Showtime.*

That night, he tossed and turned in a strange mix of fear and excitement. When he dozed off after midnight, the phone's ringing woke him.

The voice was familiar. "I know it's you, Sameer. Stop this nonsense, if you know what's good for you."

"Ketan, I don't know what you are talking about. I…"

"Think of the girls."

The Ketan who spoke to him on the phone was different from the man he had known. Gone was the suave, polished CFO, who always said the right things at the right time. This was a desperate man whose world was crumbling around him. Sameer got up and checked the locks on the front door and the balcony, and then watched over the sleeping girls. He couldn't wait for the night to be over.

At the break of dawn, *Financial News* arrived – dynamite wrapped in a rubber band. 'Stonewell Board involved in Insider Trading', screamed the headlines in bold. Nikhil Roy told the entire story as it was, no punches pulled. Management decision to include Biochem results in Stonewell financial statements prior to the public issue and Board and management colluding on profiting from the spike in share prices. He even included the mail from the irate Board member who hadn't sold off his shares in time.

Sameer checked his cell phone every few minutes. The girls were home; he continued with the curfew despite their whining. At lunch time, he poured rice and daal on his plate, but couldn't eat.

It was four in the afternoon when Roy finally called, "Gokhale resigned. Moral responsibility."

He sat down, covered his face with both his hands and took a deep breath.

From there onwards, the actions were swift.

The *goras* stepped in for damage control. The Board was dismissed, Srini and Ketan fired. A temporary Board was constituted, comprising clean names from business and civil society. London assumed control of management and a few ex-pats were assigned top management jobs for an interim period.

Simultaneously, SEBI, the stock market watchdog, swung into action. It decided to launch a fresh enquiry into the scam. Bansal, Srini and Ketan were held for questioning and later arrested.

The girls went to school the following day; the black Scorpio was gone.

The glass button with the number seventeen glowed as Sameer pressed it. It felt strange to be going back. *To the office.* He had never thought he would return. But there he was, making the vertical journey in this metal box.

Tim Reyonlds, Global Financial Controller of Stonewell, was visiting India and had asked Sameer to meet with him.

He had always hated the routine of getting up every day and going to the office. And then, when it got taken away from him, it was the only thing he thought about.

The sliding door flew wide open, as if in welcome. As he entered, he thought he had come to the wrong floor. The reception area had been transformed. There was a new mauve and cream carpet, with spherical design, flowing in a rhythm. Stonewell colours. Sectional sofas and stylish cast-iron, glass-topped coffee tables had replaced the old furniture. A flat screen television beamed stock market news.

Mitali greeted him from behind a new mahogany desk.

Sameer needed to wait a bit; Tim was finishing up with another meeting. It felt odd sitting at the reception as a visitor.

He thought about his team. Kartik had been fired for his complicity in the scam. However, Arjun, Neha and Neena were still around.

Tim Reynolds came out, tall and lean in a dark suit, his hair nearly all white. His smile was warm and his handshake firm.

Tim had been at Stonewell a long time and had risen through the ranks; he was well respected amongst peers and colleagues. He was a known India fan – with an appreciation for her culture and people. Crazy about Indian food. Sameer remembered the last time they had all taken him out to Kareem's a few years ago. He had enjoyed the food – *sheermal, korma, kebabs, sikandari raan*. They had ended the meal with a *paan* from a shop nearby. There was a mix up and Tim had ended up with a tobacco one. It had taken hours for him to recover from the 'boom boom in his heart', as he called it. They had laughed together afterwards. The India-loving gora suddenly not so sure about all things Indian.

Tim took him to Ketan's old office which Tim was using. Everything there had changed too. Ketan's photographs and the certificates on the walls were gone, replaced by paintings and Stonewell posters. The furnishings were an extension of the colour scheme of the reception area.

Tim was a direct, no-nonsense guy. The pleasantries lasted only a few minutes, before Tim got to the point of the meeting.

"Sameer," said Tim as he got up to shut the door, "We feel foolish for our misjudgment on the financial statements mess. With the benefit of hindsight, we should have investigated when you were implicated. But we didn't suspect Ketan could misuse his powers like that. The Board members' involvement, we hadn't even imagined."

"I understand how you would've misread the situation. Ketan was, *is*…," he smiled as he said that, "a smooth operator."

Tim shrugged. "He'll get what he deserves. But it'll take a long time to build back our credibility."

"You've made a good start. New Board, new management team."

"We're doing all we can." Running his fingers through his hair, he asked, "Anyway, what're your plans? Have you started working elsewhere?"

"I'm talking to a few people… but nothing has firmed up yet."

Tim leant forward towards him, "Sameer, we'd like you to come back…"

Here it was finally. Vindication. Sweet. Just.

"…as the CFO of India operations."

What?

Tim rambled on about the company needing a strong and stable person and how they valued his knowledge of India operations. Sameer only half heard him. Stonewell was offering to take him back to be *CFO* of the company. He had come hoping to be offered his old position. If he got lucky, he had told himself, he may even be offered the Controller's slot. But CFO – that was beyond the realm of his thoughts.

Of course, during his career with Stonewell, he had imagined it. The peak, the crowning glory of his life. Becoming the CFO of Stonewell. The one crore plus salary club, the company Mercedes, fifty people reporting to him.

Tim had stopped talking and looked at him.

Suddenly, Sameer knew what he wanted. Unintelligibility of his own desires had been a problem; he had often wanted what others expected him to want. Not any longer.

"Tim, I'm overwhelmed by your faith in me. However, I'm afraid… I can't accept your offer."

Tim looked surprised. Clearly, he had done his homework. He knew Sameer didn't have another job yet. "Sameer, if it's a question about compensation package, we can discuss. We can match an offer you may have."

Sameer smiled. "Quite the contrary. The offer I have, the *only* offer I have, would pay me less than Stonewell did."

"I don't understand."

"I didn't either. Till now. Here I was, being offered far more than I expected… and I realized I don't want it any longer." Sameer leant back in his chair. "The thing is, Tim, I am done with Stonewell. In fact, I am done with the whole business world, this culture of chasing bottom lines, making more money than you need, and becoming a Ketan in the pursuit. Long hours, killer deadlines, and ruthless competition. I am done with all that." He squared his shoulders. "My priorities have changed. My kids need me more than before. I'm a single parent now."

"But you're in the prime of your career. Surely you aren't contemplating retirement?"

Sameer shook his head. "No, I can't afford to. But I don't want another monster job that'll consume me and leave no time for home. "

He looked at the Stonewell poster behind Tim. Two happy kids playing with a toy car with three bottles of *Tiny Colds* displayed at the bottom (*now in three flavours – cherry, grape and bubble gum*). "I have an offer from an NGO that works for improving the lives of street children. They need an experienced professional to manage their finances – to make optimum use of their limited resources. That's what I'm going to do."

Sameer smiled. "The money is less, but enough to get by."

Tim smiled back. "You seem to know what you're doing, Sameer. That's something."

Sameer laughed. "I hope so." He hesitated for a moment before speaking, "May I ask you for a favour?"

When Tim nodded, he continued, "We have an office boy here. Ashok. He's a high school graduate and has been with Stonewell for over twelve years. A dedicated, committed worker. He could do more. Perhaps be a Stores Assistant or something."

Tim jotted down Ashok's name on his pad. "I have confidence in your judgment, Sameer. I'll see what I can do."

Tim got up. "Well… won't hold you for too long then. It's our loss, Sameer. But you know where to come if you ever change your mind."

Sameer got up to shake his hand. "Maybe we can go out for lunch before you head back for London. Still fond of Indian food?"

Tim held a finger up. "No paan this time."

Sameer laughed. "No paan."

Namastey London

The train came to a halt with a hiss and the sliding doors opened. Ritu followed Aayush inside. He found them a seat by the window. A desi middle-aged woman opposite them glanced up from the book she was reading and gave Ritu a warm smile. Seven months pregnant, Ritu was used to the reaction and smiled back.

The pregnancy hadn't been too bad except for the swollen feet at the end of the day. The fortnightly health check-ups had all gone well. Both the baby and she were doing fine.

Aayush peered outside the window, unceasingly amazed by London sights. She liked London. There was an order to everything. Traffic on the roads, signs at the grocery store, queues at Starbucks. No homesickness so far – there was too much of India there for that to happen.

One thing she didn't care much for was the weather – the rain and the cold. They had moved at perhaps the worst possible time, right in the middle of winter. For the five minute walk from her apartment to the Tube station, she dressed in layers of clothing – overcoat, gloves, cap, scarf, earmuffs. And yet when she arrived at the station, she was a mess; watery eyes, running nose, chilled to the bone.

She was enjoying the summer though.

Aayush continued to look out of the window. She didn't know how much he understood about the baby that was on the way. They talked almost every day of what was to come, but she wasn't sure how much he comprehended. She wondered how would he be with the baby, how the baby would affect him. His teachers said it might be good for him, could teach him compassion, responsibility. She hoped they were right.

She squirmed as she felt the baby move. It could be a bit disconcerting if it happened when she was lost in work, the baby kicking her back to the reality of the life within her.

"Aayush?"

He turned towards her and she noticed the appearance of the fuzz above his lips.

"The baby moved again. Do you want to feel it?"

This fascinated him, she knew. He nodded.

She took his hand and put it on her belly. A few moments later, the baby obliged and Aayush smiled.

The Royal Academy of Music had given finesse to his playing. There was flair to his performances. His teachers in Delhi had taught him all they could. But it was more technique than creativity. Here, they had set him free. He was encouraged to make his own music. Without rules, without boundaries. And he thrived in it.

A concert was coming up the following month. A big event, with the Mayor and a cabinet minister expected to attend. There would be a session with Aayush playing with a few of his autistic classmates, all budding musicians like him. And they would start with a piece composed by Aayush. She had cried when Aayush's teacher told her.

The baby moved again and brought her back to the present.

She had been able to persuade her parents to move to London. They'd be here for her when she delivered. Government of India would finally get possession of the flat Mr Kedar Nath Srivastava clung tenaciously to, for twenty-five years.

She missed Sameer. There were times when she wanted to pack up and leave, just to be with him. But she knew she couldn't. Sometimes when they talked, however, she could feel the distances shrink. Who knew what the future held. For her. For him. For the baby.

Wake Up, Sameer

❁

They were at the dining table and Ammaji had served dinner. Green beans-potatoes, arhar daal, rotis and rice lay steaming on the plastic table cloth of bright orange flowers of an unknown and probably unreal species.

"Can I go first today?" Tania asked, looking at Sameer.

"It's my turn," responded Pari, raising her hand.

"But I have something important."

"Me too. It's breaking news." She turned to Sameer and began before the argument could go any further. "Dad, you know Srishti…"

"No, I don't know Srishti."

"LOL. Loser." Tania laughed.

"Daddy!" Pari whined. "The big news is that Srishti is going out with Ankit."

He had rolled up his kurta sleeves and was putting rice in his plate. He stopped mid-air. "Let me get this straight. We're talking ten year olds. Right?"

"Right."

"And Srishti and Ankush are *going out?*"

"Srishti and Ankit. Not Ankush. I don't even know who Ankush is."

"Ok. Ankit. Let's focus on Ankit. We'll discuss Ankush another time. So Srishti and Ankit are *going out?*"

"Yes."

"How do two ten-year-olds *go out*? *Where* do they go out?"

"I don't know." She shrugged her boney shoulders. "They hang out at school. Richa saw them holding hands once."

He looked at Tania in consternation. "Hmm…interesting. Are they planning to marry anytime soon?"

"Don't be silly. They're only ten." Pari rolled her eyes.

"Apparently ten is not too young to be going out," he retorts.

He reached home around six on weekdays. Tania was usually studying. Pari barely gave him time to change his clothes before she started to talk. They went for a walk in the park together and she talked nonstop, bursting with news from school. And yet she had more stories to tell at the dinner table.

He turned to Tania, "Now, it's your turn." He got up and switched on the air conditioner; it was too hot. Even the frowning tribal woman in the painting seemed to be sweltering.

"Are you sure? She may have something else equally *important*." Tania said, making air quotes.

He looked at Pari and smiled. "I'm sure. Besides, Pari and I can always talk later. You're the busy one."

"I had my meeting with the school counsellor today."

How could I have forgotten that?

"She has suggested a few other schools to check out in US and UK."

He had taken too big a morsel of rice and vegetables. He shook his head and chewed quickly before he was able to say, "With your grades, you should find a good college in Delhi University."

"It may not be easy. The cut offs are going up each year."

"I'm sure you'll make it. You can go to US or Europe for your Master's, if you like."

She nodded.

He didn't want Tania leaving too soon. Her post-graduation was four years away. He'd have time to prepare for it.

His job at *Purpose International* was going well. They never had someone with his experience and they were impressed with his ability to leverage their limited resources.

At home, they had to cut back a little. He sold the Maruti Zen Kavita used and Dayal was given a tearful send off. Sameer was a bit more conscious of the cost of things these days. But overall, it wasn't too bad.

One of the perks of the job was that he got to switch off his computer at half past five every day and head home. In time for the walk-talk with Pari. The weekends were free. It felt liberating. He was enjoying his time with the girls.

He looked towards Pari. "It's time you started eating, darling. Tania and I are almost done and you haven't even started."

"I hate beans."

"You hate everything that is food and is green."

Pari made a big show about cutting a piece of her roti, dipping it into the sabzi and putting it into her mouth.

Dinner conversations were back to how they used to be years ago.

Except for the empty fourth chair.

When the kids had gone to bed, Sameer lay alone, and thought of Ritu. He imagined her bustling about in the office, busy.

Unable to sleep, he got up to check on the kids. Lights in Tania's room were out. He went into Pari's room and sat down on the edge of the bed to watch her sleeping under the glow of her night light of constantly moving stars. At her bedside table stood a picture of Kavita, Tania and Pari he remembered well. He had taken it on the garden of their hotel in Goa. Kavita lay on her stomach on the grass, ten-year old Tania on top her and two-year old Pari on top of Tania. Kavita was pretending to be crushed as Tania and Pari looked up at the camera in laughter.

Sleeping, Pari looked serene, radically different from the animated daytime Pari. She shifted and her hand landed on his. He caressed it and she smiled in her sleep. He wondered what she was dreaming about. She had told him of her last; she had been in a sunny garden where the birds sang and the flowers danced. The difference was that the singing and dancing was literal. The flowers jumped around in the flowerbeds in amazing dance moves and the birds took song requests to sing popular Bollywood tunes. That's what Pari's dreams were like.

Kavita had written a poem about Pari's dreams and Pari had been crazy about it. She had Kavita read it to her every night. He had an urge to read the poem right then. Back in his bedroom, he opened the locker in Kavita's cupboard where she kept all her poems, and amongst the notebooks lying there, found what he was looking for. He went back to Pari's room and recited the poem to a very asleep Pari.

When you are sleeping

When you are sleeping
I love to watch you
To tuck away the few errant strands of hair behind your ear

Now don't get me wrong
It is not that I don't like you awake
But your being asleep is something special
You look so peaceful when you are sleeping
That I feel peaceful just by looking at you
You know, perhaps we should show pictures of you sleeping on
the TV
Our contribution to world peace.

I often wonder about your dreams
Your dreams must be fun too

Wish I could climb behind your closed eyelids
And watch these dreams with you
Like a cinema hall
With just you and me

So again, don't get me wrong
I love you awake
But I love you a wee bit more
When you are sleeping.

He looked at her. She was oblivious to him and his reading of her favourite poem. The delicate fragrance of the jasmine wafted in from the open window. They were in full bloom. He tucked an errant strand of hair behind her ear, kissed her lightly on the forehead and walked out of the room.

Everything in his room was a memory of Kavita. The dresser with her lipsticks, eye shadows, compacts, eyeliners, perfumes. They seem to be an extension of her – her eyes, lips, face. And those tiny beautiful boxes she collected from everywhere, lacquer, papier-mâché, marble, carved wood. He picked up the carved sandalwood one they had bought in Mysore and ran his fingers over the carving; it was chipped at the bottom from the fall it had years before.

As he opened the locker to put back the poem, on an impulse, he took out all her poetry notebooks. The identical covers of tiny blue squares were smooth to his touch. He counted six volumes.

He picked one on the top. It had a neat index in the beginning, marking name of the poem, page number and the date of the writing. He thumbed through it idly, stopping to look at a few of them, written in Kavita's neat hand.

Perhaps he could show these to the editor of the magazine she wrote for. Perhaps, they could publish them as a book. *She would like that.*

The last volume took him by surprise. It wasn't poetry. It seemed to be a sort of diary; he hadn't known she kept one. However, the first half the notebook was torn out, only a few middle one written on and the rest of the notebook blank. It was as if she had destroyed parts of the diary that were more than a few days old. *Strange.* For a moment, he debated if he should read it; if she would've wanted him to. Then curiosity got the better of him as he looked at the first entry – August 22, 2013 – four days before she died.

It was about her father; she was concerned about his health. She was planning a trip with the girls to Chandigarh and Ludhiana to see her father and Nandita.

He flipped to the last written page and spotted his name.

As he read, it was like each word was a tiny dart targeted to numb his brain, take away his ability to think and leave nothing behind but white noise. The shock was sudden. Blood drained from his face and he could barely hold the notebook in his hand.

One solitary page written the day before her death.

August 25, 2013

Today, I thought about the why of what happened. Between Sameer and that woman. I am no longer obsessed by it; do not spend entire days thinking about it. It hurt badly then, like someone had driven a steel rod right through my chest and forgotten about it. The feeling of inadequacy, the self blame, the shame. But those days of pain also led to some helpful analysis. I rode out the road of self blame. Sameer had no right to cheat on me, to make a mockery of our marriage of eighteen years.

There was no excuse for the deceit. But I reached a point where I could forgive Sameer.

Back to my reflections today. I think it happened because Sameer is forever searching for happiness he thinks his present does not offer him. A promotion. A bigger car. A lower golf handicap. Another woman. What he doesn't realize is that the box of happiness he's looking for doesn't exist. If only he focused on what he has. A loving family, a successful career that has always given us more than we need. If only he were to look within. He would know he has what he seeks. And more. As Guillaume Apollinaire put it, 'Now and then it's good to pause in our pursuit of happiness and just be happy.'

Will that happen? Will he look within? That's the question.

If I am such a know all, why don't I share this 'gyan' with him? I did that many years ago – but like most of us, Sameer doesn't learn through discourses. He figures out the right way of doing things by making mistakes and learning not to make them again. I only hope he does it sooner than later.

Wake up, Sameer.

Acknowledgements

There are a number of people I want to thank, who started me on this journey and supported me each step of the way. I'm sure they understand they can't all be named.

My parents – Sushma and Late Dr. R.K. Narula, for their indulgence for my adolescent writing.

Late Surinder Gulati, for his legacy.

My early readers – Sandeep Jain, Hena Kanungo, and Chaya Khanna – for reading frenzied gibberish and still finding encouraging words to say.

Manjul Bajaj, for her insights into the publishing world.

Arup Bose and Dipti Patel, for their faith in me.

Stuti, for a meticulous job in editing the book.

The two people I love the most in the world – Mahika and Eeshma Narula, for allowing me time on weekends (away from Monopoly, Blokus, and Rummy-cube).

And finally you, the reader, for choosing to read this book even though you were spoilt for choices.